Washington Square Secrets:
Book 4
BETRAYAL

By Carrie Dalby

Book designed and published by Olive Kent Publishing
Mobile, Alabama

Original watercolor on the cover by Amanda Manley
Title and chapter fonts in Yataghan—Regular
carriedalby.com

One

Ernest Abbott grinned at the wide-eyed stares his little brother and Arabella Harrington gave him as he made the doll dance across the veranda without touching it.

When Arabella's doll curtseyed, Baxter clapped.

"Do it again, Ernie!" Baxter jumped to his feet from where he had sat spellbound on the woven rug.

Laughing, Ernest shook his head. "I promised Clive I'd meet him in the greenhouse after lunch."

Arabella gently scooped her doll off the table where Ernest had made it lay using his telekinesis. She inspected the doll's pale limbs and the soft fabric of her torso under her ruffled dress.

"It's all right, Arabella," Ernest said. When her hazel eyes looked up from beneath her straight, brown bangs, he continued. "I didn't hurt her, I promise."

She clutched the doll to her chest without speaking.

"Will you do more magic for us later?" Baxter asked.

"Sure, Bax. But I'll need to pick something else to use. I don't think Arabella liked sharing her doll."

She turned away, still clutching her toy.

"It's okay. Ernie didn't hurt it." Baxter's arm went around his friend's shoulders. Arabella was a year older than him, but she didn't seem to mind being comforted by a five-year-old.

Ernest followed the flagstone path through the garden. The July sun immediately made Ernest's scalp burn along his left-side part as much as the stones heated the soles of his bare feet. He ran a hand through his blond hair to get it off his forehead as he crossed next to the patches of blooming sorrel and yarrow. At the greenhouse, Ernest pulled out his handkerchief and wiped the sweat off his neck. Clive Harrington's curly blond head was bent over a tray of herbs he was thinning at the workbench.

"You must sweat five pounds off in here every day," Ernest remarked. "No wonder you're so skinny."

"It took you long enough to get here," Clive said without looking up.

"Bax and Arabella wanted another magic show." Ernest perched on the empty stool near the bench.

"Your card tricks and levitating chairs this morning weren't enough?"

"I guess not." Ernest reached out to grab a hand trowel from the table. He used the metal edge of the tool to clean a bit of dirt out from under a fingernail.

"Hey!" Clive snatched it. "Go up to the house if you feel the need to groom."

Ernest kicked his feet against the stool's crossbar. "I said I'd help you and I will."

"Then don't bother cleaning your nails. If you help me separate out these parsley plants for my mom, we can check the new pond plants sooner." Clive placed a cluster of the greenery into an empty pot.

"I can do that without getting my hands dirty."

"Not with my plants, you don't." Clive's glare was icy.

"Wouldn't it be gentler on them than handling everything?"

"Not if you do it properly."

Ernest rolled his eyes. Clive was pretentious about all the plants on the Harringtons' property, bragging when he discovered new ways to get them to grow heartier. Sure, he had a hand in caring for them, but it was Clive's mother who put them to functional use. Miss Jo created teas and other concoctions to aid healing for people—including Ernest's own adoptive mother after she had lost a little girl born too soon a couple years back. The brightness in her eyes had dimmed and not even her husband could make her smile. But after several weeks of his mother partaking daily of Miss Jo's herbal tea crafted especially for her, she began to act like her old self.

After observing what Clive was doing with bare hands, Ernest lifted the nearest clump with his mind.

"Don't they teach you how to follow instructions in that public school of yours?" Clive swatted at Ernest, causing him to lose control of the parsley. It fell on top of one of the other plants with a scattering of soil.

Ernest stood. "Sure they do, but that doesn't mean I'm going to take directions from a thirteen-year-old."

"You should if they have superior knowledge."

"Get over yourself, Clive. If it wasn't for your plant knowledge, you'd be on the same level as everyone else. Worse, actually, since you can't throw a baseball."

"There's more to life than ball games. If you're so grown up at fourteen, you'd know that."

Ernest stomped out of the greenhouse. Hearing the voices of Clive's little sisters and Baxter coming from the new pond, Ernest went to the house for some peace. Spending a couple days a week in Spring Hill with the Harringtons had been fun the past two months because Miss Jo had trained him how to utilize his telekinesis. Before then, he had only accidentally used it when scared. Now that he had control of things, he was able to practice anywhere. He didn't need Miss Jo's instructions, especially if it meant putting up with Clive, who'd grown loftier as the humidity continued to rise. Clive was a younger version of his father on the outside, but where Mr. Harrington only looked like he felt superior to others, Clive acted on it with his arrogant attitude.

As he approached the back of the house, Ernest heard his mother laughing.

"And then," Miss Jo said, "he remarked that I'd been wearing trouser longer than most women in Mobile, but I still wore them best. I told him I had my clothing hand-tailored, which hides subtle flaws. And *not* so subtle, which I added while patting his bloated middle."

"You did not!" His mother looked incredulous when he stopped on the edge of the veranda.

"I certainly did, which I followed up with the statement that he was nowhere near the shape of the man I used to swoon over in the boxing ring."

"The judge is still as handsome and charming as ever, and you know it, Josephine."

"Everyone else tells him as much," Miss Jo said with a regal wave of her iced tea glass. "Sean needs all the humbling reminders I can offer."

His mother smiled as she turned to him. "Hey, Ernest. Is everything all right?"

He shrugged and dropped into the nearest chair.

"Do you need a drink?" Miss Jo asked.

Her blunt bangs and freckled face reminded him of Arabella's uncanny gaze after he'd made her doll dance. "No, ma'am. I'd rather be in town playing ball with Theo and Jack."

"Ernest!" His mother exclaimed as a blush brightened her cheeks.

Miss Jo laughed. "Don't fault him, Fran. I'm glad he feels comfortable enough to be honest with me. Did you and Clive hit a rough patch?"

"It's always the stupid plants with him. He never even breathes a word about girls, let alone baseball."

"Would you like to see what you can do to help Sarah in the kitchen with your skills?"

Ernest shook his head over the idea of using his telekinesis to do the Harringtons' housework. "No thanks, Miss Jo. Mom, could I take the streetcar back to town and meet up with my friends?"

She glanced at Miss Jo.

"Don't be so formal, Fran. Y'all are like family and those ridiculous society codes your mother drilled into you aren't in play at my house. I'll not force Ernest to stay when he'd be happier elsewhere."

Her brown eyes flickered from her best friend to Ernest.

"Please, Mom? I'll be home before dinner."

She sighed. "Get the necessary tokens out of my purse."

Ernest sprang out of the chair and kissed her cheek. "Thanks!"

Miss Jo laughed.

"And thank you, Miss Jo."

Half an hour later, the breeze through the open streetcar windows cooled Ernest's face as the trolley sped down the tracks on its descent into Mobile. The closer they got to the river, the heavier the air felt.

Once he was off the Spring Hill line, Ernest detoured to Royal and Dauphin Streets, to the tallest building downtown. A quick look in the soda fountain on the first floor of the eleven-story Van Antwerp tower showed a smattering of familiar faces, but not the friendly one he sought. Those enjoying the cool marble décor and ceiling fans were people who typically snubbed him, so he continued south two more blocks.

At Government Street, he waited in the shade of a nearby awning with half a dozen other people for the next streetcar to stop. When he heard the rumble of a motorcycle, he shifted to stand behind a large woman holding a Hammel's Department

Store parcel on one side and a little kid's hand on the other. A Western Union telegram deliverer zipped by on a motorcycle. Ernest smiled to himself and stepped out from behind the woman. Then his adoptive father, Jim, pulled his Harley-Davidson to the curb.

"I thought y'all were at the Hill today. Where's your mother, Ernest?"

A Mobile Police motorcycle was enough to grab people's attention, but the sound of Jim's deep voice held even the toddler captive. His booted foot rested on the curb as he balanced the bike awaiting Ernest's reply, mustache twitching with each passing second.

"She's at Miss Jo's for a couple more hours," Ernest said. "I got permission to meet up with Jack and Theo."

He nodded, the sunlight glinting off the silver eagle medallion on the crown of his hat. "And she and Bax are well?"

"Yes, sir." Ernest shied from the others watching their exchange.

"I'm glad to hear that." Jim's gaze switched to the people lingering in the shade. "Are you waiting for the streetcar, ma'am?" he asked of the woman with the toddler and package.

"Yes, officer."

Jim nodded toward Ernest. "That's my son, Ernest. He'd be happy to carry that parcel for you."

Ernest mustered a smile as he turned to the woman. "Yes, ma'am."

She handed over her package while smiling more at his father than him. Ernest had hoped it was a hat box, but it was too heavy to merely hold a frilly head covering.

"Thank you, officer. I'm glad to know there are still gentlemen these days. You're a fine ambassador for our city."

Apparently the compliment was enough to break through the layer of fatigue Jim had carried the last few days because a grin brightened his face. "Thank you, ma'am. Y'all be safe. I'll see you tonight, son."

Ernest breathed a sigh of relief when his dad tipped his hat and continued down Government Street.

"You must be mighty proud of your father," the woman said to Ernest as she lifted her child to her hip.

"Yes, ma'am."

"I used to think the traffic officers were a nuisance with their noisy bikes, but when my cousin came into town this Easter, she was smitten with them. She said every city needed a handful of dashing officers to keep drivers on their best behavior."

Ernest nodded, relieved to see the approaching streetcar and the freedom it offered. But when they boarded, Ernest's jaw tightened at knowing he was stuck with the chatty woman since he held her box. He reluctantly sat beside her. The child immediately started banging on the package lid.

Without missing a breath, she tucked the kid's hands into her own. "There's nothing so handsome as a man in uniform." She paused long enough to study Ernest. "I must say, you don't favor your father, but you look familiar. Do you look like your mother?"

"Yes, but I'm adopted, so you don't know her."

"I should have known that good officer would rescue as many people as possible after the way he took care of me. You're a lucky boy."

Lucky my parents died in a murder-suicide? "Yes, ma'am."

"A fortunate boy, that's for certain."

Hoping to be rid of her before long, Ernest adjusted the parcel on his lap. "Which stop is yours, ma'am?"

"Monterey, on the southern side of Government."

Ernest inwardly groaned at having to ride all the way around The Loop with her. "Do you need assistance to your door?"

"No, but it's kind of you to ask. That father of yours raised you well."

By the time she exited with her toddler and parcel, Ernest was ready to scream. Another minute of her gushing about Jim would have sent him over the edge. At least there weren't any other teenagers on the streetcar. The feeling of being judged when others knew your dad was a cop was the worst.

Antsy from listening to the woman, Ernest disembarked at Ann Street and walked toward Hartwell Field in hopes of finding Theodore and Jack.

By the time he'd gone half a dozen blocks, his shirt clung to his sweaty back. No sounds of wooden bats hitting balls or shouts of players reached his ears. Only the whistle of a train from the railroad tracks that ran on the far side of the field. When he was close enough to the baseball park to see the only people there were a group of four boys his age or older leaning against the fence in the shade, Ernest made a left onto Virginia Street to go home. Without turning around, he knew he was being watched.

Then followed.

Ernest cussed himself for not staying on Government Street. He could've walked by the Melling mansion in hopes of spying Lousia Davenport on one of her regular visits there. Instead, Ernest cut through Magnolia Cemetery—the shortest route to George Street since he could climb the iron fence if the northern gate was shut.

"Come on!" A voice called behind him. "I bet the other gates are locked!"

Ernest wanted to run, but knew that would be the worst thing to do.

Footsteps on the gravel road behind him grew closer. Ernest refused to turn. When the steady pace changed to running, he took off like an Olympian.

He was fast, but when Ernest cleared the final plot and jumped at the fence, a hand gripped his ankle before he could pull himself over the top.

"Gotcha!"

Ernest found himself face down on the grass with a couple guys sitting on top of him.

"Where's Ryan?" someone asked.

"He said it was too hot to chase anyone."

"He never left the field?" the same guy questioned as a knee went into Ernest's back. "You better tell him it was me that caught 'em."

"Yeah, but it'll be me that clobbers him."

There was a scuffle, then the squirming weight was off Ernest's back. He was yanked to his feet at the same time a punch landed in his stomach. Before he got his hands up to defend himself, another struck his cheek, then a second to his gut.

"Hell, it's that murder kid!" The biggest boy backed away. With the others watching their friend, Erenst studied his surroundings for something he could use as a weapon.

"He murdered someone?" the skinniest asked.

"His old man did. And there's been talk about some weird shit happening around him this summer. I bet he's haunted."

"You scared, Scotty?"

"Maybe." The fat kid straightened. "You would be too if you knew his old man killed his mama before blowing his own brains out."

Fear could be leveraged. And a haunting.

"You come here to visit your mama?" the skinny one asked Ernest as they all stared at him.

Nodding, Ernest pointed to a nearby plot that had a shepherd's hook with silvery bells hanging from it. The metal began swaying in the windless air, chiming a ghostly tune.

"See, he's haunted!" The big one shuffled back.

"Mama, help me!" Ernest shouted as he caused the nearest gravestone to teeter.

The marker fell onto the grass with a thud that shook the ground. Suddenly pale in the heat, the three boys ran toward Hartwell Field. Ernest grinned after them before climbing the fence.

Two

Jim Abbott jerked awake with his face pressed against the ceiling. The fan whirled in the late July heat, rhythmically slicing through his legs without slowing.

"Damn." He had woken up outside of his body again, as he had every morning since his thirty-second birthday the previous week.

Before Jim could force his spirit back into his body on the bed below, he drifted through the ceiling and above the trees. The Washington Square neighborhood slept under the oak canopy north of Magnolia Cemetery, the housetops like stones in a bed of moss. To the east, downtown Mobile gleamed in the dark oasis of pre-dawn, the city shining brighter than the fading stars. It was an amazing sight, but Jim didn't have the reserve strength to lose key hours of sleep while exerting himself to return to his body. Especially during the blistering summer when he worked all-day patrol shifts.

Spying the bell tower of the police station, he yearned to keep drifting so he could permanently escape the stern eye of the police chief. Jim hadn't gotten a promotion in forever, and the house felt smaller each year. The false freedom astral projection offered faded with the thought of his family. The image of Francesca and their boys was all the motivation he needed to trudge through another day of traffic patrol. Seven years ago, he had worked hard to win Francesca's heart and would never leave her. Their adopted son, Ernest, was developing into a head-strong young man who needed a father around. Not to mention their youngest, Baxter, was growing daily and eager for learning. Jim wanted to witness each day of their lives.

As though swimming through a haze, Jim's astral form attempted to reunite with his physical self. Concentrating on the house, then the unseen room below the roof, he shifted through the dense atmosphere until he was back where he begun. Fortunately, he'd managed to return home quicker than he had the previous nights.

From above, Jim gazed at his wife's arm across his bare middle on the double bed and smiled. Francesca's gray cat, Rochester, was curled on her pillow on the opposite side. The sheet was kicked off and Francesca's thin nightgown allowed him to peruse her figure before focusing on her lovely face. Her six years of seniority never bothered him, but after she had miscarried their last child two years previous, Francesca had blamed her age and fell into a quiet depression that lingered long after the initial loss.

That is, until Jo Harrington discovered Francesca was still sulking.

At the beginning of summer, Francesca's best friend had mixed an herbal brew to get her "back in balance." Over the past month, Francesca's brown eyes shone with love and laughter like the days before their heartache. If drinking a couple cups of daily tea was what it took to keep his wife healthy, Jim was more than pleased for Jo to do her witchy magic.

But it was with Jo that Jim had first experienced astral projection. It wasn't anything he wanted to try again—especially unintentionally each night. Jim knew he could no longer put off speaking to Jo about his accidental astral wanderings, but he didn't know how he could fit in a trip to the Harringtons' house in Spring Hill without worrying Francesca.

"Jo can keep this unholy venturing. I don't want it," he muttered as he threw himself into his body.

The feeling of Francesca's heat branding him where they touched highlighted his success. Jim eased away, wanting to rise without disturbing her.

"Jim." She breathed his name as her hand went to her chest with a slow caress.

Not wasting the opportunity of a fevered dream, Jim stroked her bare arm. "My Francesca."

She stilled, and the cat jumped down from her pillow.

"I'm here." Jim's touch ran the length of her arm before settling on top of the hand at her breast. "You needn't dream when I'd do anything for you."

He lowered his lips to hers. She yielded, mouth warm and welcoming. Her touch trailed his abdomen, arousing him with the sensation of her soft fingers.

Awakening fully to the primal groan of his want, Francesca leaned away, brown eyes wide.

"Fran, it's all right." Jim kissed her neck. "You were dreaming of me."

She nuzzled his shoulder as she hugged his middle. "For a moment I thought I was still slighting you."

"Those days are in our past," he whispered. "My woman who loves to touch, dance, and make love is back."

"I'll never be able to make up those months to you."

Jim took her by the hips and pulled her on top of him so he could hold eye contact. "We were together in our home every day with Baxter and Ernest. Being with y'all is what's important to me."

The edge of her bobbed brunette hair brushed the corner of her lips as she looked down at him.

"And don't start harping about your age. You're only two years shy of forty but sometimes speak as though you're a shriveled old woman." Jim caressed the curves of her backside. "Not that I've felt up old ladies, but I'm sure we can safely say you feel nothing like someone past her prime."

Her broad smile brightened the room as much as the rising sun. Jim grinned in return and Francesca fingered the dimple in his left cheek before smoothing his mustache.

"I love you, Jim. Thank you for taking care of me and the boys."

He let out a half-exasperated sigh. His previous worries about Francesca's well-being had faded, but concern over Ernest falling into danger because of his abilities had taken their place. The summer of 1927 was proving to be one of frenzied hatred. Central Alabama was ripe with vigilantes wearing white robes and masks, flogging people in the name of God who didn't act in a way they thought proper. Not to mention the violence among the youth in their own city and rumors of northern mobsters staking claims along the Gulf Coast.

"I'm doing the best I can, baby," he said to Francesca. "If I ever make detective—"

"I'd miss seeing you on the motorcycle."

Laughing, he gazed at the provocative way she bit her lip, a flirtatious gleam sparking in her eyes. Jim knew Francesca took pride in his job though she prayed daily for his safety while he was on patrol—especially after two police officers had been killed in the line of duty in the past few years. He hugged her tight and rolled so they were on their sides, facing each other.

"I love you, Francesca. I just wish I could get a promotion so I could give you and the boys a little more than what we've got now."

"We don't lack anything, Jim. And if we need something extra, there's always the money my parents left." Her hand rose, fingers brushing his jaw. "I know you don't like dipping into that, but what's mine is yours—ours."

"I'd rather you saved that money for things for yourself, baby, like when you hired Cyrus to decorate the parlor or buy new dresses for the season."

Francesca nipped his neck and whispered, "and those pretty lingerie sets?"

"Especially the silk and lace." He kissed her mouth as his hands roamed over her thin cotton gown. "I'd like to spend all day like this, but I need to get ready for work. I've yet to sufficiently impress Chief Burch, and reporting to the station late on a morning the traffic officers have a meeting won't do me any favors."

She raised her eyebrows hopefully. "Tonight?"

"Nothing will stop me then."

By the time Jim had showered and dressed in his riding pants, boots, and shirt, Baxter was playing in the hallway.

"Morning, Bax." Jim hoisted the five-year-old and tousled his hair—the same rich brown hue as his mother's. "What's with the fancy sailor suit?"

"Mommy's bringing me downtown for new shoes." Baxter poked at the bit of gauze covering a nick on Jim's jaw from his shave.

"You don't want to wait until my day off tomorrow?"

"Mommy said you're taking me fishing, so I need my shoes today."

"That sounds like a smart plan, son. I'll see you in the kitchen."

Jim paused outside Ernest's room before opening the door. At the foot of the bed Sunny, the orange tabby, lifted his head and then lazily tucked back down. Jim scratched behind Sunny's ears, nudged Ernest's arm, and waited.

"Breakfast."

The teenager grumbled and pulled the sheet over his head.

"Don't make your mother wait, son."

As soon as Jim stepped into the hall, the door shut firmly behind him. He expelled a frustrated breath to keep from yanking the door open to tell Ernest not to use his telekinesis to backtalk. If it had slammed... but fortunately it hadn't.

"Ernest's attitude is getting too big for his britches," Jim said as he entered the kitchen. "I think I preferred when the telekinesis only manifested when he woke from a nightmare."

Francesca, wearing one of her pretty blue dresses typically saved for Sundays, met his gaze. "He's becoming self-assured, which I appreciate."

Jim knew there was nothing more unruly than a headstrong young man. Add in the fact that Ernest had special abilities, and all Jim could see was a recipe for disaster.

Francesca laid out eggs, toast, bacon, and orange juice for everyone, plus a cup of coffee for Jim on the kitchen table. Jim sat close so they could work the crossword puzzle in the newspaper together. They took turns filling in the squares and talking with Baxter about what he wanted to do in town. When she wasn't actively writing letters on the grid, Francesca rested a hand on Jim's thigh, a simple gesture he had missed during her depressive state.

Ernest finally joined them when they were halfway through. He was dressed for a day outdoors.

"Morning, Ernest." Francesca kissed his cheek when he sat on her other side, across from Jim.

"Thanks for breakfast, Mom."

"Baxter needs new boots," she said as he dished up. "Do you want to go downtown with us?"

"I'm going to Hartwell Field."

"With who else?" Francesca asked.

Ernest shrugged. "Theo and Jack and whoever wants to join us."

"Is there a baseball game?"

"Not this morning. We'll make our own in the side lot."

"Would you like me to pack food for you? Baxter and I might eat downtown."

"I'm not a baby, Mom," he said with annoyance.

"No, you're not." Francesca smiled with pride. "I'll give you fifty cents, should you need it. Be home for dinner."

Even after the adoption, Ernest had called Francesca "Miss Fran" until Baxter was big enough to say "Mama." He had switched to "Mom" as though he wanted to remind her that he was her son, too. But Jim was still Jim, the only change from the early days when Ernest had called him Officer Abbott. It stung after all those years that Ernest didn't openly admit Jim's status in his life, but he would never force it.

"Don't forget our fishing trip tomorrow, Ernest," Jim said.

"Yes, sir."

"Are you coming, Mommy?" Baxter asked.

"Maybe in another month or two, when it's cooler," she paused to wipe a bit of egg off his cheek, "but I'll see you off with a full picnic basket."

When they finished eating, the boys scattered. Jim dressed in the rest of his uniform, then cornered Francesca by the sink, hands smoothing over her hips as he leaned in for a kiss.

"If I'm downtown after my meeting, I'll keep an eye out for you."

She straightened his bowtie, traced the winged wheel patch on the jacket sleeve of his upper left arm, and then touched the shield-shaped badge pinned to the front of his jacket. "And I'll watch for your motorcycle, Officer Ninety-six. Be safe, and remember I love you."

"I love you too, babydoll."

Jim went through the back porch and passed his pickup truck on the side of the house at the same time Ernest jumped down the front steps holding his baseball mitt. Ernest ran to the Reardons' yard across the street. Jack Reardon joined him, a baseball bat in hand. The bat quivered before springing out of the boy's hand and into Ernest's waiting one six feet away. Laughing, they ran toward Palmetto Street.

Jim grimaced. He knew Ernest wouldn't keep his secret from his friend, but if he was doing things like that where anyone might see, word was bound to get out. Ernest and his pals were already ostracized, and Jim didn't want any more stigma placed on them. Having been orphaned because of a murder-suicide when he was seven was more than enough for a boy to endure. Ernest didn't need to draw attention from something as unexplainable as telekinetic power, especially in the current social climate.

As for his friends, Jack was soft compared to his hotheaded older brother, and Theodore Farley was every bit as awkward as his math teacher father—but without a record-breaking college football career to boast about. Add in Theodore's notorious mother, Deborah, who communed with ghosts, and the eldest Farley was doomed from the start. Fortunately, between Ernest, Jack, and Theodore, they weren't often outnumbered enough to be heckled.

"Lord help the fool who ever picks a fight with Ernest," Jim muttered as he thought of the way Ernest had subdued his father's ghost seven years ago. One of his biggest fears was Ernest turning into William Hart—menacing and cruel in both life and death. Jim was doing all he could to see that Ernest was raised properly so there wouldn't be room for what might remain of his old family's blood.

When Jim reached the trolley stop on Government Street, Deborah Farley was waiting with her youngest.

"Good morning, Miss Deborah."

Her smile melted into a frown as she turned. "Whatever is the matter, Jim? Your aura is scattered." Besides being a talented medium, Deborah also had the gift of seeing auras. "You must have a lot on your mind, though there's a pink blush at the edge of it."

"Yeah," he smiled sheepishly with the thought of his loving encounters with Francesca, "some aspects of life are great while others are troublesome."

"It weakens everything in you physically, mentally, and spiritually when you're off-balance. Talk to Josephine as soon as possible."

"I already have plans to, Miss Deborah," Jim said as the eastbound streetcar came to a stop.

He boarded without having to surrender a token as uniformed officers rode for free. Once Deborah was seated, he stood watch over his neighbor as the other passengers eyed her with curiosity or disdain until he exited at Royal Street. Jim walked a block west to the police station on St. Emanuel. He did his morning round of greetings before settling in the conference room with the handful of other officers assigned to motorcycle duties as part of the Traffic Unit. At the top of the hour, the shift lieutenant and chief of police stood in front of them. The lieutenant reviewed department policies and an increase in speeding violations around the city before starting in on the growing problem of youth gangs.

"There were groups of rowdy boys on the south side when I was in school," Jim said. "It's nothing new."

"As I recall, Abbott, you were one of the hooligans," Officer Murphy joked, causing the other officers to laugh.

The chief cleared his throat.

"There have been reports of theft, destruction of property, and women being harassed. I want it stopped, and I want the residents of those areas to see as many patrols by the Flying Squadron as their typical beat men." Chief Burch looked around the room, eyes falling on Jim. "Abbott, since you come from that stock, you should be able to root it out. Focus your patrols south of Government Street unless you're asked to go elsewhere. Harper and Stout will also focus on that area. Get them boys to see sense before they turn into career criminals."

"Yes, sir." Jim was glad his deep voice didn't reveal his concern over the weight of the responsibility.

"Murphy and Green can focus on the youth activity in the north during their patrols. We get more reports about the boys there at night, especially in the alleys of the business district."

"Yes, sir," Officer Murphy said with a smile. He was four years younger than Jim and excited to be on motorcycle detail. Everyone called him Happy because day or night shift, he was always grinning.

As they were finishing up, a call came in about a multi-vehicle accident on Broad Street near Springhill Avenue.

"Help control the crowds over there, Abbott," the lieutenant commanded. "You can patrol the south side this afternoon."

An ambulance was already on the scene when Jim got to Broad Street, but he was the first reinforcement for Officer Fitzwilliam, whose beat it was in. The passengers and drivers were hauled to the nearby hospital, yet the looky-loos interested in the metal carnage persisted. As the hour passed, sweat beaded Jim's forehead beneath his hat as he kept the spectators back from the wreck. He thought the trucks would never come to collect the broken automobiles, and when they finally did, the wait to get the vehicles hooked up took even longer.

It was past noon before he could step away. He knew he had missed Francesca and Baxter in town, but Deborah's reminder that morning brought purpose to his lunch break. After a call into the station, Jim headed west.

The ride up Old Shell Road into Spring Hill was cooling. When he climbed off the bike in the Harringtons' driveway, all three children waited for him.

"Hey, Mr. Jim!" Sage, the middle child, jumped for a hug while Clive, the eldest and only boy, reverently touched the handlebar of the Harley-Davidson.

"Hello, Sage." Jim removed his gloves and smoothed her wild curls before smiling at Arabella. She was a miniature version of her mother in looks, though their personalities were nothing alike. "It's good to see y'all. Before you ask, Clive, you can't take it for a spin."

The oldest Harrington laughed. "Have you let Ernest drive it?"

"Nope, so don't get any ideas." Jim pocketed his gloves. "Is your mother home?"

"Where else would I be on a day like this?" Jo called from the front porch. "There's no better place to be than The Hill in the heat of summer."

"It does feel a heap nicer than town. I know Fran and the boys have enjoyed their visits." Jim climbed the steps to the brick mansion. "I don't have long, but I need to speak with you."

"Come in." Jo kissed his cheek when he got to the threshold. "Are you on your lunch break?"

"What I need to discuss is more important than food."

Jo tsked. "Sarah! Jim's here and needs something to eat and drink, please!" she hollered as she steered him to the library.

"I didn't mean for—"

"Stuff and nonsense." Jo nudged him into the darkened room that caught the breeze coming through the veranda on the backside of the house. "I won't have you fainting from lack of nourishment. Now disarm yourself and relax."

Jim smiled at her bossy insistence and slung his holster over the back of the desk chair.

Then Jo was before him, going at his row of jacket buttons. Once his jacket was on the chair with his holster, he hugged his wife's best friend. "Thank you, Jo. Thank you for everything you've done for Francesca."

"All is well now, right?"

"With Fran, yes." He sat on the chaise. "But I've got a few problems."

Jo sat beside Jim, her freckle-dusted face turned towards him. "What's wrong?"

"Ever since my birthday, I've woken with my face pressed into the ceiling. It's like that time you pulled me out of my body to show me what my mind and spirit were capable of, but when I realize where I am, I panic."

"And you float further away?"

He nodded. "It takes forever to gain control of the situation."

"Your spirit is revolting from the stress in your life by escaping. When is the last time you expanded your aura?"

"Months. Maybe a year."

"Denying your abilities is dangerous. Not only does practicing keep your spirit in balance, it ripples through all aspects of your life. Have you been clumsy lately? Suffering stress at work?"

Jim laughed. "I'm a policeman—every day is stressful. But since you mention it, I've been nicking myself when I shave, and work is a drudgery. The heat while I'm on patrol seems worse, I can't get a promotion, and Chief Burch seems to have taken a further dislike to me than he had in the beginning."

"We'll blame that on Judge Spunner since Burch is repressing everyone who's friends with the previous two chiefs and their corrupt circles. Spunner had you fixed in their sights for making detective. The current chief won't do it anytime soon just to be contrary."

"But there's room since Detective Callaghan moved to Montgomery last month. Everyone knows I'm the only one interested in the position."

"Don't take it personally, Jim. Enjoy being one of the elite members of Mobile's Flying Squadron while you're young."

"That's one way to look at it, " he said with resignation.

"The only way. Besides, I know you ate up the attention you received from that newspaper article about you this spring when it called out your status as the senior motorcycle officer and that you cut a figure that any—what was it? 'Any girl would swoon over.'"

Jim laughed. "That anyone could *respect* because of the way I handle traffic issues. It was Harper and Green who got called out on how well they look in uniform."

"You're none too shabby yourself, Jim," Jo said with an impish smile.

Sarah, the Harringtons' mature housekeeper, arrived with a tuna and cucumber sandwich tray and a glass of lemonade. Jim thanked her and took a few bites before speaking again.

"I saw Deborah this morning. She told me my aura is scattered."

"It's no wonder since you're denying it. Take time to meditate and expand your aura. Francesca will understand your need to momentarily focus on that rather than her, and if not," Jo said with a wicked grin, "you can join your aura with hers while you're actively engaged in physical pursuits."

Jim laughed and then drank half the lemonade.

"Cyrus loves to watch me when my astral form is wandering," she went on. "He says it's the only time I look angelic—when my devilish spirit is away."

"I don't doubt that. But you think expanding my aura a few times a week will cure me of the floating issue?"

"Most likely, but it might take several days for you to regain full balance. Speaking of skills, I've been wanting to test Ernest with astral projection."

Jim straightened. "He has enough to handle with his telekinesis, and if I'm having this problem because you disconnected me once seven years ago, I don't want you messing with my son!"

"Don't blame me for your troubles. Those are on you for neglecting your soul. Besides, Ernest's been doing well with everything else I've tutored him about."

The image of Ernest taking Jack's baseball bat from half a dozen feet away blazed through Jim's mind. "What the hell have you been doing with Ernest?"

"Teaching him what he's capable of. He's well over fourteen. It's high time he knows that the powers he possess are gifts that can be used every day rather just in fear."

"That's dangerous, Jo. You remember how things went out of his control the year his parents died. He nearly burned his house down!"

"Only allowing him to lash out when he's emotional is dangerous. He needs to see the good and practice it so there isn't a repeat of those events."

"You need to stop. If Francesca knew about it, she'd say the same thing."

"Fran knows and thinks it's wonderful."

"Then why hasn't anyone bothered to tell me?"

"You'll have to ask Fran. Since you declined my invitation to host you for your birthday dinner in favor of the Patersons' offer, I haven't seen you in months." Jo's tone conveyed she was hurt by the snub, but the Patersons had been his friends longer than the Harringtons. "Ernest put on a magic show for everyone the last time they were here. His control is marvelous. He's at that age when a young man needs to feel secure about something in his life."

Jim stood. "And what do you know about young men in the real world, Jo? Do your experiences with your silver-spoon husband give you that insight? Or is it from your private school son that lives in a mansion with a witch for a mother?"

"Don't you dare speak like that about my family!"

"And don't corrupt mine with your fantastical ideas." Jim yanked on his jacket.

"Ernest needs this, Jim. Talk to him about your aura. You can bond with him over your capabilities to protect loved ones. You've protected Ernest that way at least once." She laid a hand on his sleeve. "He'll understand."

Jim flinched away from her. "It was never spelled out for him."

Jo motioned to his revolver as Jim buckled his holster. "Your job is to keep the peace in Mobile. Ernest has the potential to protect the whole city single-handedly. He's old enough to understand that weight and respect it. Clive and

Sage were told of my astral and telepathic skills when they each turned ten. That's when their tutoring began. Both can call out to me from as far away as school. And with only a few months' practice, Sage has proven an accomplished astral projector as well as telepath. It's their right to utilize their God-given strengths."

Jim scoffed at her brazenness. "God-given, is it? It sounds more like Josephine Harrington bestowed. Do what you want with your own children, but stop playing goddess with mine!"

"If you deny Ernest support, you're going to devastate him more than William Hart ever did."

"If you were a man, Jo, I'd bust your face for that remark."

Jim's boots solidly struck the hardwood floor the length of the hall as he stalked out. He pulled on his gloves, mounted his motorcycle, and kick-started the engine with brute force—revving out of the driveway without a backwards glance.

Three

Jim stepped off the streetcar and started into the neighborhood as he lit a cigarette. He automatically waved and called "good evening" to neighbors sitting on their porches, but he didn't stop to chat as he often did. On George Street, he paused under the oak in front of the house to finish smoking. He had calmed in the hours since he left the Harringtons' house, but he wasn't looking forward to confronting Francesca about why she hadn't told him Jo was tutoring Ernest. Since it wasn't a conversation they could have at home where the boys might overhear, an evening drive would be the way to handle it.

After dropping his cigarette butt in the porch ashtray, Jim smoothed his mustache and opened the screen door. Rather than calling out, he silently hung his hat on the coat rack before stopping in Baxter's doorway.

"Daddy!" He left his pile of blocks to hug Jim. "We didn't see you when we went shopping."

"There was an automobile accident I had to help at."

"Did anyone die?"

"Fortunately not, but people went to the hospital, and there was a big mess to clear." Jim squatted in front of Baxter and felt the leather boots. "Those look sturdy. Are you ready to go fishing tomorrow?"

"Yes!" Baxter hugged him. "Will we get to see the sunrise?"

"You bet we will." Jim hugged him back and tousled Baxter's hair. "And I've got a feeling you're gonna catch your biggest fish yet."

In the bedroom, Jim tucked his Colt revolver into his top dresser drawer and changed into a pair of trousers, suspenders, and a shirt he left opened at the neck. He put on his loafers and pocketed his truck keys so he would be ready to leave after dinner.

Francesca was at the kitchen counter, mixing crumbled bacon into a bowl of cold pasta salad.

Jim came up behind her and encircled her waist. When he felt her tense, he knew Jo had telephoned. A kiss on the shell of her ear helped her relax.

"Hey, babydoll."

"Welcome home, Jim." She leaned back and turned her head to kiss his cheek. "Baxter and I missed you this morning, but when I heard about the automobile accident, I figured you'd been called to attend it."

"I was. Could I bring anything to the dining room for you?"

Francesca motioned to the lettuce and tomato platter. "Thank you."

Ernest came in the back door as Francesca was pulling the sweet tea pitcher out of the refrigerator.

"You're just in time. Please get washed up," she said.

"Yes, ma'am."

When Ernest walked by Jim in the hall, he smiled at his son. "Did you have a good day?"

"Yes, sir." He kept moving, but Jim put a hand on his shoulder.

"I'd like to take your mother for a ride after we eat, so I need you to take care of Baxter. See that he gets a bath and everything. You can listen to all the radio programs you want, but don't stay up too late. We've got an early morning tomorrow."

"Yes, sir."

Ernest continued down the hall, and Francesca met Jim's gaze with a questioning eye.

"We need an evening out together," he said as they went to the dining room.

Baxter kept the conversation at the table active with his excitement over the fishing trip. After the meal, Francesca asked the boys to clear the table. "I'll wash the dishes when we get home," she added.

Jim waited for Francesca in the front hall. When she returned from their bedroom, her bobbed hair was shiny from brushing.

They held hands on the way to his Model A pickup. When he pulled onto the street, the crunch of the gravel ruts marking his parking space drowned out the sounds of the cicadas. He drove southwest, enjoying the wind coming in the open sides beneath the canvas top.

At a quiet curve along Dog River he had found on one of his fishing expeditions, Jim cut the lights and engine. The utter darkness engulfed the Ford like their silence had on the drive.

Francesca turned to Jim. "Josephine said you were upset."

"I'm not mad at you, Fran." He shifted from behind the steering wheel on the bench seat, knees brushing his wife's as he turned to her. "I'm disappointed that after all we've been through you didn't share something this important with me."

"I know how exhausted you've been with your patrol duties during the heat. I had hoped Ernest could surprise you on a day you needed a distraction."

"Jo has no business leading Ernest on with promises of unlimited power and whatever other magic she's peddling."

"It's not magic. Ernest is capable already, she's just teaching him to hone his skills. He can handle things as small as a dime to as large as a dining table for minutes at a time now."

"What good will that do him in the real world?" Jim threw his hands up in a gesture of disbelief. "He can't go through life relying on telekinesis. Ernest needs to deal with honest labor, rejections, and pride in accomplishments properly earned."

"And he can do all those things along with understanding his abilities. He's still carrying the weight from his father's actions. I've seen it in his eyes, but it's lightened since he's been meeting with Josephine. He feels a sense of worth about himself that you or I could never give him." Francesca rested a soft hand on Jim's forearm. "Jo knows the soul. To be successful in life, Ernest has to believe in himself. Jo's helping him do that."

"But he's being reckless. He took Jack's bat from six feet away right there in front of the Reardons' house where anyone could have seen it fly to him."

She sighed. "Jo warned him about that. I'll talk to him."

"No, I'll speak with him. He can't be doing that out in the open when vigilante Klansmen are hunting anyone different."

"I thought that was all up north."

As soon as he saw the fear on her countenance, his arms immediately embraced her. "I don't mean to scare you, baby, but things aren't right around here either. I'm keeping an eye out as best I can, but I need to know everything that's going on with the boys, okay?"

Francesca nodded, but worry still painted her face.

"We're a team, Francesca. I know Jo's been in your life longer and we owe her a lot, but when it comes to the boys it needs to be us."

"It is, Jim. I never meant to keep it a secret from you forever, just until the moment was right."

Jim nodded and enfolded her in his arms. "And I appreciate your concern over me. I have been tired lately, and this summer seems hotter than ever. I'm sorry my temper's been short."

Innocent kisses meant to comfort were peppered across her forehead like the stars shining above the tree line. Francesca nestled under Jim's chin, and he kissed her hair. She looked up at him as her hands trailed his suspenders. With a flirtatious smile, she playfully settled on his lap.

"You want to, baby?"

"You promised me tonight. Remember?" Her dark eyes were luminous in the night as she worked open a few of his shirt buttons. "And we've never done it in an automobile."

"We sure haven't." Jim grinned as he felt up her bare legs, searching beneath her dress. When he reached her naked backside, he paused.

"I had hoped we could enjoy the privacy when you mentioned a drive. I've been thinking about it since you bought the truck last year—our first vehicle."

The truck rocked and they panted in the sultry night. Jim added to the heat when he expanded his aura and fused it with Francesca's. The complete connection sent her over the edge with a keening cry that silenced the wooded area around them.

"My love will always surround and fill you, Francesca."

A deep, searching kiss further linked them as he reached his own pinnacle.

"It gets better every time, Jim," Francesca whispered as she rested on his shoulder. "I love you."

"I love you too." He held her to his chest "And I've wanted you like this since the moment I saw you."

"Sweaty and half-naked down a dark lane?"

"At least twice a day, babydoll."

Francesca laughed as she smoothed her dress. Jim fastened his clothes before sliding back to the driver's spot for the return ride to town.

At home, Jim settled cross-legged on the parlor rug beside Ernest, who was stretched out as the hum of a radio medley closed out a program. Jim reached over to click the machine off. The number dial slowly dimmed.

"Did Bax get to bed?"

"Yes, sir." Ernest sat up and moved so his back was against the mauve sofa, not making eye contact.

"Thank you for watching him. Your mom and I needed some time together." Jim studied Ernest's profile. Soft chin, rounded nose, cold blue eyes under a flop of dark blond hair he'd grown out that summer. "Remember when we saw Babe Ruth play that exhibition game at Monroe Park?"

He looked at Jim. "How could I forget?"

"You said it was the best day of your life, and that you were glad I'd brought you."

Ernest nodded.

"And that you were happy we were a family." Jim paused, focusing on the love he felt and allowing it to warm his chest and spread outward. "I've been pleased to be with you from the beginning of this family's origins. I love you more today than I did the day of the adoption, and I want to be sure you know that. I'd like to think I show you, but I know things can get awkward as you're growing. You're nearly half my age now. That gap is gonna keep closing and I hope I'm on the inside of it when you catch up to me. I have the feeling you're going to surpass me, son."

"Surpass you how?"

"With strength, intelligence, and skills." Jim grinned. "And probably with the ladies too."

Ernest dropped his gaze, but there was a whisper of a smile on his face.

"You got your eye on a girl this summer?"

"Yes, sir."

"Don't go trying to impress her with your telekinesis. I saw what you did to Jack's bat this morning. You need to be more careful. I found out today that Miss Jo's been teaching you how to work your ability, but you need to be discreet when you're not at her house. There's too much at stake."

"Like what?"

"Haven't you noticed the flogging headlines in the newspapers the past month? You need to be careful about your reputation, not to mention stigma that might be cast at your mother or your little brother."

"Or you?"

"I'm the last one to worry about, Ernest. I can hold my own but a woman's character is important in social circles, not to mention Baxter is at a tender age. You know what it's like to struggle with friends from when you were little." Jim laid a hand on Ernest's knee. "Harness your skills, as Miss Deborah always taught you. Ground yourself. Don't flash it around as a show of superiority."

"You don't understand what it's like."

"I do, Ernest." Accepting Jo's suggestion of bonding with Ernest over their gifts, Jim focused on his love. The warmth in his chest expanded out. Ernest looked around as though trying to understand the shift in the air. "Do you feel something?"

"It got hotter."

"That's my love for you manifesting through my aura."

Ernest leaned away. "Like what Miss Deborah sees?"

"Yes. She watched me protect you from a malevolent spirit when—"

"From my father that time after the fire when Aunt Narcissa was here." Ernest stared at Jim as though seeing him in a new light. "You saved us."

"Yes, and I'd do it again if needed—for you or any of my family."

"Is that what Miss Jo taught you? She told me she used to tutor you."

"My ability was there, like yours was, but I learned to control it after training with her to combat my shell shock, and seeing how Deborah works."

A pensive look filled Ernest's face. "Why didn't you tell me?"

"I didn't think you needed to know, but I was wrong. You should've known I understand what it's like to be able to do things others can't."

"But what I do is different. People can see the results."

"Which makes it even more important to guard."

Movement out of the corner of his eye caused Jim to turn. The red porcelain rose he'd given Francesca for their fifth anniversary hovered in the air rather than sitting on the piano where it was typically displayed. It was one of Francesca's most prized possessions and she always warned the boys against touching it. Anger that Ernest dared to play with it dispersed when Jim noticed he wasn't being careless. His full concentration seemed to be on the rose. It drifted directly in front of Jim. He raised his hand to catch the delicate sculpture.

"Well done, Ernest." As Jim finished the words, his revolver floated into the room. He set the rose on the floor and scrambled to his feet. "You're not supposed to touch that!"

"I'm not." He looked disappointed Jim wasn't impressed, then turned hard. "And I didn't touch Mom's flower either."

"This isn't a joke, Ernest." Jim snatched the Colt and tucked it into his pocket. "I want you to promise never to do that with either of these things again."

"I promise." Ernest stood, making them nearly eye to eye because only a couple inches separated them in height. "And I'm sorry, Jim."

"All right, son," he said through a tightening jaw. "Goodnight."

Jim watched him leave, then replaced Francesca's rose on the piano with a huff. He picked up the framed family portrait that was beside the flower. On Ernest's twelfth birthday, they had gone to Eric Overbey's Dauphin Street studio to capture the special day. Three-year-old Baxter happily sat on Francesca's lap, covering the roundness of her middle. Ernest perched beside them and Jim stood behind the trio, a hand on the shoulder of each Ernest and Francesca. Ernest smiled, looking forward to their next stop at George's Candy Store. Francesca glowed with serenity, thinking another baby would soon join their family. Every time he saw the picture, Jim thanked God none of them knew what would happen a few weeks later when their daughter was born too early.

By the time he showered, Francesca was already asleep. Jim stretched out on the bed beside her and stewed over the worries that Ernest could now control multiple things at the same time, including what wasn't in his immediate area. It might not be the ultimate power he voiced concern over with Francesca, but it was beyond anything Jim had fathomed.

Four

A shaft of light from the hallway widened until it reached Ernest's face when the bedroom door opened. Sunny stretched from his spot at the foot of the bed and jumped down.

"Time to get up, son."

Jim's deep voice and warmth caused an instant flood of comfort over Ernest's sleepy mind.

"Baxter's already eating, so don't be long."

Ernest waited until his father turned away before pulling on a pair of denim pants. He left his bedroom light off and fumbled for a shirt until he remembered he didn't need to physically struggle for what he wanted. Straightening, Ernest opened his hand and concentrated on the green shirt. A second later, the clothing exited the closet and dropped into his hand.

When he came out of the bathroom, the aroma of bacon and maple syrup filled the air. His mother made pancakes before every fishing trip. It was one of Ernest's favorite routines, and he knew he'd never grow out of it.

"Morning," Ernest said to everyone as he took his seat at the kitchen table.

"Good morning, son," his dad said over his coffee cup.

Baxter smiled as he chewed a mouthful of pancakes.

Their mother brought over a steaming stack and slid them onto Ernest's plate, kissing his forehead in the process. "Morning, Ernest."

"Thanks, Mom."

Besides the pancakes, the other good thing about their pre-fishing breakfasts was that they were quiet. There weren't any crossword puzzles for his parents to discuss because the morning paper hadn't been delivered yet. No chatter unless Baxter was doing it. Ernest used the time to study his family, attempting to figure out how he fit into the Abbotts when he'd been born a Hart. They all had brown hair, the color of pine tree bark or darker while his was more like a water oak's trunk. Francesca's eyes were deep and large like a deer's. While Baxter's eyes weren't as green as Jim's, you could tell they were father and son. And his hair matched Francesca's perfectly, not counting the few strands of gray above her ears no one ever mentioned.

Ernest was glad his blond hair was darkening, but his blue eyes did him no favors. Only when his aunt, Narcissa, visited did he feel a kindship, the truth of his origins. The memory of William Hart loomed larger each year, worrying Ernest that his blood might be poisoned beyond any healing his new parents could offer.

When Baxter ran to get his boots, Jim helped Francesca carry their dishes to the sink. Jim encircled her waist and kissed below her ear, causing her to shy away as though it tickled. Even if he couldn't see auras like Miss Deborah, Ernest felt the strength between them. Pervasive love that knew no bounds. The air warmed as Jim continued to hold her. Ernest wanted more than anything to ground himself there as Miss Deborah had taught him years ago, but he hesitated. He was other, not Abbott.

A boot-clad Baxter clomped into the kitchen and threw his arms around Ernest. "Are you done eating so we can go?"

"Yeah." Ernest stood.

Not wishing to intrude on their parents' connection, Ernest sent his plate, fork, and glass across the kitchen. Spying the objects out of the corner of his eye, Jim took a step back to watch. Ernest's mom glanced first at the sink where the dishes softly landed, then at Jim as though to gauge his reaction, but he gave no hints.

"Y'all have fun." His mother kissed Ernest's cheek before he could retreat. She then took Jim's hand. "Take care of our boys."

"I always do, baby."

Ernest stepped away when they kissed, but Baxter joined the trio, arms hugging their mother goodbye while her lips were still pressed to Jim's.

Ernest exited the back door and took the middle of the bench seat in the pickup. Baxter curled on his lap with his feet toward the passenger door so they wouldn't be in their father's way. The rumble of the Ford's engine and the darkness allowed his brother to fall asleep within the first few miles.

Some mornings Ernest nodded off too. Today he sat erect, his shoulder brushing against Jim's on the bumpy roads outside of town. Travel smoothed once they reached Bay Shell Road along the water.

"I didn't want to bother you and Mom while you were saying goodbye," Ernest said once the road noise quieted. "That's why I brought my dishes to the sink like I did. I wasn't trying to show off, but I interrupted you anyway."

"It's no bother, Ernest. And I'd rather you use your abilities in the privacy of our home than anywhere else, but the Lord knows I'd kiss Francesca all day if I could."

"I'm glad Miss Jo helped Mom," Ernest said.

Jim patted his closest knee. "So am I, son. I'll always be grateful to her for that."

"And I'm glad she's helped me too."

"I hope you'll keep what I told you last night in mind from now on. So much can go wrong if—"

"Yes, sir."

He knew he shouldn't have cut off his dad, but he didn't want to hear about it. Ernest wasn't going to let situations more than a hundred miles away stop him from protecting himself like he had in the cemetery the other afternoon.

When Jim parked the truck, Ernest nudged Baxter's shoulder. "Time to unload, Bax."

They set their folding camp chairs above the reach of the highest tide, piling their picnic basket, tackle boxes, lanterns, and gear beside them. Their footwear was soon off, pants rolled to their knees. The sand was cool between Ernest's toes, helping reduce the weight of the humid pre-dawn air.

Baxter went to grab a pole.

"Not yet," their father said as he set down the lantern. "The tide's coming up. It's time you learned to gig flounder. Ernest, show him how to handle a pole."

It took several minutes for Baxter to get a decent grip and make quick stabbing motions with the prong-tipped gig. The flare on their dad's cigarette barely illuminated his face, so Ernest couldn't read his emotions. Their dad didn't make any suggestions as Ernest encouraged Baxter to repeatedly jab the pointed end into a mound of earth. When he approached with a bucket in one hand and the lantern in the other, they both looked up.

"That's fine, boys."

They waded into the water, their father holding up the lantern to broaden the reach of the yellow glow. The first ten minutes were filled with missed jabs and disappointed sighs. Then Ernest attempted what he'd never done before—control over a living creature.

The flounder he concentrated on acted like it was having a fit. Once he was able to hold the fish stationary in the tide, Ernest made it swim under the area Baxter was hunting. It took his brother two stabs, but he squealed with delight as he raised the gig.

"Look, Daddy!" He waved the pole that was taller than himself toward their father before swinging it towards Ernest. "See what I did?"

Their dad's smile was just as large as Baxter's. "Great job, Bax! And you, Ernest, for teaching him."

Their father held the bucket under the pole and had Baxter slide the fish off. Baxter went right back to work—and so did Ernest. He made a pretense of trying to gig a few for himself, and barely nabbed one, but having to concentrate on the fish for his brother left no room to keep trying for himself.

When Baxter had nearly filled the first bucket, their dad called Ernest over. "Take this in and get an empty one."

"Yes, sir." Ernest took the heavy bucket and passed his gig to him.

Baxter caught nothing when Ernest was on errand, though their dad guided him and gigged his own one-handedly.

"Good job, Daddy!"

Ernest held the bucket for him to offload his flounder, but he didn't offer the gig back to Ernest once he was relieved of it. "You're on bucket and lantern duty, and *nothing* else. You don't want to overdo a good thing, son."

"Yes, sir." Ernest relieved his dad of the light.

Herding fish was a lot more trouble than he expected, and Ernest was happy to rest his brain. He gazed at the bay as it turned rosy gold. The gentle flow of the tide sparked a trail of diamonds along the miles that separated them from the Eastern Shore. Louisa Davenport's family often visited across the bay with the Mellings, who had a weekend house on the cliffs near Montrose. Ernest only went over the bay once a year when his family vacationed at the fancy hotel in Point Clear— Francesca's favorite getaway. But he could imagine the way Lousia would look in a sporty swimsuit, auburn hair loose in the wind or tucked under a bathing cap.

When they switched out the gigs for fishing poles, their dad stood between the boys as though that would stop Ernest from assisting his brother.

"What are you going for, Daddy?" Baxter asked.

"Reds. What about you?"

"Big ugly reds!" Baxter jumped up and down, splashing water.

"Hey, Bax. You know better than that. You'll scare the fish away."

But Ernest already had a redfish swimming right for Baxter's hook. A few seconds later, the boy's line gave a mighty tug.

"Fish! I got a fish!"

"Not yet you don't," their dad said with a chuckle. "Remember, you've got to reel it in and get it from the hook to the bucket before you can claim it."

Focusing on the hooked fish a dozen feet away, Ernest let it struggle so his brother would have a legitimate fight for it.

"That's it, Bax! Slow and steady." Jim coached as Baxter cranked the handle on his reel. "Now slowly back yourself out of the water toward the collection bucket."

Baxter stumbled and landed on his backside in ankle-deep water, but managed to keep hold of the rod and got on his feet without fussing. His thin arms strained as he reeled and tugged for another minute before the fish was in shallow enough water for them to get a good visual on it.

"It's huge, son! Keep working it."

Their dad shoved his own pole into the sand and watched Baxter with his undivided attention. That allowed Ernest to wiggle the fish's tail for show as it crested the bay.

"I got it!"

"Almost, Bax." Their dad followed him in case Baxter asked for help. "Get it to the bucket before it flops off the hook."

Baxter triumphantly raised the bucket holding his catch while his dad unhooked it. After Baxter reeled in his third big one in a row, their dad sat in the sand with a cigarette between his lips, letting the boys do their own thing. Ernest concentrated on helping Baxter until they stopped at nine to eat.

"You're doing a great job, Bax," their dad said as the boy devoured a sandwich.

"Ernest is helping!"

"I know he is." Their father's tone was flat, but he managed to smile. Though he never called him out, Ernest knew he was concerned, possibly disappointed. But Baxter's joy over the bucketfuls of fish was worth any talking to he was gonna get.

Before noon, he called the boys over.

"Y'all got more than enough to feed us, Miss Eilands, and the Patersons for a week. I'm calling it a day." Their father raised the brim of his hat with his wrist and wiped his handkerchief across his sweaty forehead with his other hand. "Start packing."

On the outskirts of town, he parked in the shade beside a general store.

"Take Bax in and get y'all each a cola bottle." He handed Ernest a couple coins.

"And one for you, Jim?"

He shrugged and fished out another nickel.

When the boys reached the door of the store, Ernest looked back. Their dad was at the payphone at the edge of the building. When they returned from the cool shadows of the store into the blistering heat, he was waiting for them in the truck.

Their next stop was Miss Eilands, the old woman Jim introduced them to the week Ernest's parents died. As Miss Eilands could never turn away a stray, she always had a litter or two of kittens around. Sunny and Rochester were acquired from her on their first visit.

Jim called out to announce them, then went through the kitchen door. With Baxter helping, their father stopped to place some fish in the icebox. Ernest continued through the kitchen to the sitting room crowded with junk, debris, and felines.

The white-haired lady looked tired, but locked her milky blue eyes on Ernest as she continued to pet the black cat on her lap. "How's that orange tabby, little mister?"

Ernest grinned. "Sunny is great, though not as curious as he once was."

"None of us are." She sighed and shifted in the rocking chair without rising.

"I caught you lots of fish, Miss Eilands!" Baxter said he ran into the room, their father behind him.

"You did?" she asked.

"Ernest taught me how. He's the best big brother in the world!"

"I remember when Jimmy taught him how to fish. Indeed I do."

Baxter put his arms around her. "Do you need anything, Miss Eilands?"

"He taught you well, little one. I appreciate the fish and hug, but that's all I need today." She stroked his hair and smiled. Then her gaze wandered back to Ernest and her voice dropped. "Don't let yesterday's good be lost in the fog of tomorrow. Stick to truths. They're like compass points and won't lead you amiss."

Embarrassed that she might understand the difference in opinions between himself and his father, Ernest mumbled "yes, ma'am" and stepped away. When he looked up, his father's green eyes bore into him with something between concern and affection.

Five

Jim was pleased to see Jo's Buick in front of the house when he returned with the boys from their fishing trip. He wasn't sure she would come when he had called her from the store since he'd left her house the previous day in a huff, but he didn't want the boys privy to the looming conversation.

After hastily searching his pocket, Jim handed several coins to Ernest. "It's been a hot day. Take Baxter and yourself for some ice cream."

"On top of the colas we got at the store when you stopped to use the telephone?"

"Yep."

"What about the fish?"

"They'll keep another half hour, but hurry back to help clean them."

As soon as the screen snapped shut behind him, Francesca called out. "Jim, you'll never guess what happened!"

He went into the parlor and looked between her and Jo. Without waiting for his reply, Francesca jumped to his side, kissed his cheek, and continued in an excited rush while holding his hand.

"Sadie telephoned. She invited us to her and Richard's new summer house near Irvington. Word is they host fabulous parties on the weekends and we're going to the one Saturday night! It's an honor to attend anything Commissioner Beauchamp and Sadie host. Deborah has agreed to have the boys stay at her house while we're gone. I'd like to make a night of it, maybe stay at the hotel in Portersville. Is that all right with you?"

"Sure, baby."

"Jo and Cyrus are attending the party as well."

At the mention of Jo's name, he held her gaze. "Do you have any idea of the potential havoc your work with Ernest is capable of?"

Jo held his stare from her seat on the sofa, waiting for Jim to continue.

"It might interest you to know your student is forcing fish onto hooks and flounder under gigs so his brother can haul them in hand over fist. It might as well have been a goddamn jubilee out there with the amount of founder and redfish they caught! We had to drop some at Miss Eiland and then with the Patersons because there was too much for us to eat within a week."

"Well," Jo said with a lazy drawl as she uncrossed her trouser-clad legs, "it sounds like an excellent lesson in helping your neighbors."

"I'd rather my boys learn about patience and be willing to share when things are tight. Not to mention I'd rather Baxter's head not be filled with the idea that everything is going to come easy to him the first time he tries something like it did with the flounder gig."

Francesca's brown eyes gazed at him with concern. "There's no harm in Ernest showing Baxter a great fishing trip."

"It's a pattern." Attempting to control his anger, Jim's voice came out in a low rumble. "I want it stopped before Ernest gets out of control."

"He needs more practice," Jo stated with her all-knowing tone. "Once it's second nature to him, it won't be as intriguing."

"I can't sit by while he's endangering himself and the rest of the family with his actions," Jim went on. "He's not being discreet, and it's only a matter of time before the whole neighborhood knows he can move things with his mind."

"Let him stretch his abilities. It's harmless fun."

"It's nothing of the sort, and I control what's proper behavior for my boys not you, Jo. Do what you want with your motley brood in Spring Hill, but I'm Ernest's father!"

"Yes, you are, Jim," Francesca said while laying a hand on his shoulder. "He might not use that name for you, but everyone knows how much you love him. We see it in your actions every day. You've been wonderful with him from the beginning. That's one of the reasons I liked you so well when we met."

"He knows how you feel," Jo added. "I've seen the way he watches you for silent approval whenever you're nearby. Respecting his abilities will get you the furthest."

Jim shook his head, not liking the uncertainty that remained after a typically joyous day of fishing. "Thank you for coming when I telephoned, Jo, but I want you gone before the boys return."

Jo hugged Jim, but he stood stiff, arms at his side. "I love you and your family, Jim. I'd never do something I thought would bring any of y'all harm."

Jim nodded, unable to speak. He went out the kitchen to the yard to set up the cleaning table in the shade. When he carried over the second load of buckets from his truck, Francesca was waiting with his apron she'd given him the previous Christmas. It was made of denim and had leather-lined pockets for scissors and knives. Jim took off his sweat-dampened shirt and hung the apron around his neck.

Francesca tied it for him, hands trailing his bare skin when she was done. She kissed one shoulder blade, then the other. Lips lingering, her hands crept around his stomach beneath the apron.

"Fran, baby, I can't right now. You feel great, but I'm not in the mood for loving."

"That's what I'm trying to change." The flick of her tongue on his shoulder did its best to switch his thinking. "You're salty."

"In more ways than one."

She sat on the swing Jim had built, watching him as he collected his filleting gear. He had a good start on the fish when the boys entered the gate.

"Mommy!" Baxter climbed into her lap. "I got the most fish ever, and had a cola and ice cream and the picnic you sent!"

Smiling, she set the swing moving with the push of her legs off the ground. "Will you have room for supper?"

"Yes! Ernest says it tastes better when you catch it yourself. I got a lot to share."

Francesca kissed his forehead. "That's great, Baxter. Be sure to help prepare them."

"He's in charge of the buckets," Ernest said as he removed his shirt. His lean body was tanned from his time outdoors that summer, his muscles strengthened enough to show a bit of definition as he reached for one of Francesca's old aprons she had brought outside.

Thinking about what Jo had said—that Ernest watched him silently—Jim reckoned he could be trying to emulate him with his wardrobe choice, though it was so hot anyone in their right mind would want to remove clothing. Despite his previous upset, he smiled as Ernest stood across the table from him and took a redfish out of a bucket. Having a hands-free option to debone and fillet the fish would be great, but Jim dismissed the thought and set his concentration on getting the job done the only way he knew how.

***

When Jim left the station on his motorcycle the next morning, he rode up to Dauphin Street and looped over to Royal as he typically did. Just before the corner of Government, a petite blonde waved him over. He recognized her silhouette instantly.

At the curb, he cut his engine. "Miss Marley, it's good to see you."

"Thank you, Ji—Officer Abbott."

"Call me Jim if you'd like."

"And call me Marie as you used to."

He smiled at the memory of the companionable hours they had spent together when he moved into the upstairs apartment from Nathan and Winnie Paterson after the war. As Winnie's best friend at the time, Marie Marley visited a lot. She and Jim were often thrown together, and he'd even thought about courting her officially. After meeting her staunch father at one of her piano recitals, Jim had chickened out, knowing his status as a new officer wouldn't be enough to impress a man who had earned his millions in timber.

"I hope you've been well, Marie."

"Yes, thank you. But I have a concern I was hoping you could help me with."

"I'd be honored to. What is it?"

Her blue eyes looked around the sidewalk, already busy with early morning shoppers hoping to beat the heat. "Could I meet you somewhere not so public to discuss it?"

"I could come by your house."

"I don't want to worry my mother."

"I'm patrolling the south side of town today. There's a little restaurant near Our Alley that has great fried chicken dinners. The tables in the side yard are shaded, and there's typically a breeze off the river. If you don't mind meeting at a place that serves all types, I could be there about noon."

"That would be perfect. Thank you."

"I'll try not to be late, but I can't guarantee my timing."

"I understand, Jim. I'll see you in a couple hours."

Jim spent his morning patrolling for traffic violations, plus chatting with business owners and neighborhood regulars south of Government, introducing himself to the unfamiliar faces and reminding the ones he already knew he'd be patrolling the area. Most had complaints about the teenagers, including several about an older teen with dark, curly hair and a penchant for causing trouble. The few times Jim caught a glance of someone matching that description, he was gone when the motorcycle turned the corner. The tell-tale rumble of the Harley-Davidson was a hindrance when trying to catch someone unaware.

He climbed off his motorcycle a few minutes after noon and raised a hand in greeting to Marie, who was cooling herself with a folding fan at one of the picnic tables under the magnolia tree. Seeing she didn't have food or drink, he went for the counter window. Jim removed his gloves as he walked and used them to sweep the road dust off his jacket.

"Your usual, Officer Abbott?" Stu, the young black man taking orders, asked. "The boss said to feed you for free because you're keeping a heavy eye on the area."

"That's mighty kind, but make it two. I'll pay the difference for my friend." Jim nodded toward Marie, who was walking up behind him, and placed the coins for her meal on the counter.

"*Friend?* Sure thing, Officer Abbott." Stu winked as he collected the money.

"It's not—"

"I'm glad you made it," Marie said when she came to a stop beside him and perused the slate board propped in the window, still waving her fan. "What are the best sides to order with the chicken?"

"It's already taken care of." Jim looked at Stu. "Holler when it's ready."

"Let me get the sweet teas now, Officer Abbott."

With the glasses in hand, Jim walked Marie back to the pine table. The only other customers in the yard were a couple dock workers three tables away, keeping with the invisible line that segregated the eating area. Jim sat across from Marie and took a swig.

Marie let her fan drop so it hung from the wrist strap and opened her purse. "Do you pay when you pick up the food?"

"Don't worry about it. They covered my meal since I'm on patrol, so I paid for yours what I was planning to pay for mine."

"That's real sweet, Jim." Marie set her purse and fan aside and held Jim's gaze with her forward manner. He marveled that she was still single when she had always been open with him. "I'm still grateful for how you got me the chance to play the organ in the Lyric Theatre back when we used to see each other more often."

"You were terrific, especially during the suspenseful scenes. I've yet to hear anything as creepy as that music. I still can't believe that horrifying tune came out of your pretty head."

"It was thrilling, as was all my time with you."

"Are you still playing the piano and organ?"

"Not publicly like Winnie does at her congregation each Sunday, but I play at home and private parties."

"Order up, Officer Abbott!" Stu hollered.

"Excuse me, Marie."

When he reached the counter, Jim leaned in the window. "Listen, Stu, don't get any ideas about this lady. She's a neighbor who needs help."

Stu handed over the forks and food, smirking. "Gals like that don't meet men in this part of town unless they have ulterior motives. And she did talk up one of the local fellas before you arrived."

"She needs police help, nothing more."

"*You're* gonna need help if your wife finds out."

Jim could hear Stu snickering behind him as he walked back to the table.

He set a plate with two pieces of fried chicken, a heap of butter beans, cooked greens, and a hunk of cornbread down in front of Marie before taking his seat.

"Thank you." After trying everything, Marie caught his eye. "It's as good as you said it would be."

"It's typically crowded, but with it being hotter than Hell, people don't have the stomach for a heavy meal come noon. If you can't eat it all, just leave it on the table. Some kids will come over and finish it."

"Really? From where?"

He thumbed over his shoulder. "They're behind that broken fence, keeping an eye out. The restaurant doesn't bother them so long as they don't come begging while people are eating. That way it saves face and the kids get a thrill out of spying."

"Are they listening to us?"

"They don't care what we say, they just want what's left. I always leave my cornbread and beans for them. If I had a big breakfast and a slow morning, I'll even leave a piece of chicken."

"You've always been thoughtful." Marie's eyes flickered down. "I need your help, Jim. I believe my sister is in danger."

He took a sip of tea. "Dr. Woodslow's wife?"

"No, not Grace Anne. Sadie—the middle one. She's married to Richard Beauchamp."

"One of our esteemed commissioners," Jim remarked, thinking of Francesca's words about him the previous afternoon. The city commissioners took turns being mayor each year, but Beauchamp—being the newest elected—had yet to hold that honor.

"Yes, but I fear he found something to make himself more money than politics, though he tends to run in both circles."

Knowing where she was headed, Jim shook his head. "No one in Mobile takes the liquor ban seriously. We've never interrupted the local runners unless the feds are looking over our shoulders. And even then, as soon as the feds are gone, the charges are dropped and the men reelected. There's nothing I can do from my end."

"I've spent a good bit of time out at Richard's country house. He acquired it from a Chicago man, complete with businesses on the back lots. The men there are dangerous," she whispered. "Sadie wants me to spend two weeks with her, but I told her I needed to come home to check on Mama."

"Then stay home."

"I can't leave Sadie out there. Richard doesn't even allow their children to stay with her."

"It so happens Sadie invited Francesca to their party Saturday night. I can look around, but it's out of my jurisdiction if I see anything."

"That will be perfect. How are your boys doing?" she asked, changing the subject.

"Real good. I took them fishing yesterday."

"That Hart boy too?" she asked with an arched brow.

Jim held back a flinch. "His name is Ernest *Abbott* and he's doing well."

"How do you do it, Jim?" She leaned across the table as though it were a secret. "How did you take in someone else's child as your own?"

"He was a lost soul in need of comfort. Anyone would have wanted to protect him."

"No," Marie said. "Not just anyone. He's a special case isn't he?"

He caught her gaze, wondering if she meant—but she couldn't.

"With what happened to his parents," he said after a pause. "Yes, it was difficult for him."

Jim felt her studying him as he finished off the rest of his tea, but he wasn't sure what her angle was.

"Well, it's been nice to catch up with you, but I need to get back to work." Jim stood from the picnic table and straightened his bowtie.

"I suppose members of the Flying Squadron are always patrolling the city. Constant vigilance against speeders and stop sign runners," she said with a near mocking tone.

"We do our best." He stuck out his hand. "I'll see you at the party, Marie."

"Until Saturday, Jim," she replied as they shook hands.

Later that day, twilight churned with the sounds of children playing and the chatter of neighbors gathering on porches. Jim and Francesca strolled west on Palmetto for an after-dinner walk, calling hello to the porch sitters that were looking toward the road and passing those facing away without disturbing their peace.

When they passed the Marleys' house at the corner of Palmetto and Roper Streets, Jim studied it out of the corner of his eye. He knew the layout because of the piano recitals the Marleys hosted for Marie and Winnie that first year he had known them. The front parlor windows were curtained, but a glow spilled from beyond, partially lighting the dining room opposite.

On Rapier Avenue, Jim stopped in front of the Farleys' house and called good evening to Alvin and Deborah.

Francesca approached the house, but Deborah left her rocking chair and hurried down the path to Jim's side.

"Your aura is still fuzzy, but it's much clearer than it was the other morning." Her tone was soft with concern while she looked up at him. "I heard from the boys the fishing was great yesterday. I'm sure the morning on the bay was refreshing for you."

Not wanting to air concerns about Ernest in front of potential witnesses from neighboring yards, Jim nodded. "Thank you for your concern, Miss Deboarh. I think I'm on the mend now."

"I'm glad to hear that. Your family and the whole community need you balanced and healthy." Deborah leaned closer. "Fran is overflowing with pink. I hope you know she always shines like that when you pass by together. Her soul soaks up every bit of love you give her."

He smiled as Francesca joined them. "Thank you for telling me, Deborah, and for agreeing to watch the boys this weekend."

"I'm happy to. And Fran informed me of your worries surrounding Ernest. You can be sure I'll speak with him."

"Great," he said with relief. "You'll be a calming influence after Jo's exhibitionism. Goodnight."

At home, they found that Ernest had orchestrated the washing of the dishes and Baxter was in the bathtub.

"Come sit outside with me," Jim told Ernest as he slipped a cigarette from his case.

"Could I have one?"

"No, and don't go filching them either—from me or anyone else." Jim sat on the top step of the front porch, Ernest beside him. "You can smoke when you've got a job and can afford to buy them yourself."

"I want to get a job. Mr. Graves said he might need me at his store after school this holiday season. Then I could get

Mom something nice for Christmas. I'd let Bax sign the package too, even if he only puts in a penny."

Jim took a drag from his cigarette. "That's good of you, Ernest. And your mother deserves everything nice we can give her, whether it's gifts or love or service."

"Why did you chase off Miss Jo before we got back from the ice cream counter yesterday?"

As long as Ernest was willing to converse, Jim would talk with him forever. "She's been a great friend to your mother since they were girls, but her opinions are often different than mine. We disagree about what's acceptable and risks verses benefits. Jo rushes in without thinking of the larger picture. I want my family members to think critically about possible repercussions rather than acting in haste. Do you understand that?"

Ernest shrugged. "Yes, sir. I guess I do."

"That's a start. Let me know if you have questions—anytime." Jim bumped his knee against Ernest's and took another drag. "I also have first-hand information about how young men act when they're excited or nervous or wanting to impress someone. At those times, it's even more difficult to think logically. That's why it's best to run things through in your mind before a situation comes up. Decide how you'll react before it happens."

"Is that what you did?"

He laughed. "Not by a long shot. I had a rough life in my younger years, but only part of it was because of my family's situation. I heaped trouble onto myself that I can't blame on anyone else."

"Did you fight?"

"Nearly every day."

"Skip school?"

"Yep." Jim exhaled a smoke ring.

"Kiss girls?"

Jim nodded. "Sure did—and more."

"How much more? And how old were you?"

"Too much and too soon." Jim ground the cigarette into the tray and elbowed Ernest. "Who do you have your eye on? A girl in the neighborhood or someone from school?"

"Neither." Ernest picked up a brittle oak leaf, crushing it between his fingers. "She lives off Catherine Street near Dauphin and went to private school, but she's starting at Mobile High School next month."

"A member of the parish?"

"She's Episcopalian, at least her father was. Her mother is nothing from what I hear."

"Nothing?"

"A Yankee nothing."

Jim snorted back a laugh. "Who taught you to talk like that?"

"That's what Tommy says about her when she comes around the park—she's a half-Yankee nothing, but she's the prettiest girl I've ever seen with her auburn hair and fancy clothes."

"What's she doing in Washington Square if she lives over a mile away?"

"Her friends live a few blocks up Government."

"Who?"

"Asher Melling and his stepbrother, Simon Campbell."

Jim whistled. "The Mellings are royalty in this town, they have been for generations. Just who is this filly?"

"Louisa Davenport."

"Major Davenport, may he rest in peace, was a credit to the Allies during the war. It's sad disease took him this spring when he'd survived being shot and every other hell in France."

"Louisa's a half-orphan. I've told her I understand about losing parents."

"Bringing up your birth parents might not be the best thing. What if she remembers the stories?"

"I'm not ashamed of my mama," Ernest whispered, "and everyone knows what happened to my family. I'm not gonna lie about it."

"I don't mean that, just that you don't have to remind people, is all."

"I'm reminded of it every day."

Jim put his arm around Ernest's shoulders. "I wish you didn't hurt so much."

"I'm not hurting." Ernest drew away and stood. "More like…."

"Scared?" Jim asked, looking up at him.

"Part of me thinks I'm gonna be like my father," he whispered.

"I'm your dad now, Ernest."

He crossed his arms, eyes glaring, but Jim could see the fear behind his pain. "Just because you adopted me doesn't mean you're my father!"

"According to the state of Alabama it does." Jim got to his feet too. "But I've loved you as my own longer than the court date, son. Think of all we've done together over the years and remember the good times."

Ernest shrugged, gaze softening.

"Playing catch, going to every Mobile Bears game possible, all the fishing trips—that was you and me, father and son, and I've loved every second of it. I wish you could see our relationship without the haze of William Hart distorting your view."

"But it's his blood in me, not yours." Moisture shone in Ernest's eyes before he shouldered past Jim to get to the front door.

Jim leaned his head back on the post at the top of the stairs and closed his eyes, allowing the sounds of the cicadas to cool the wound of not knowing how to help Ernest through his growing pains.

The slight squeal of the screen door swinging open was followed by Francesca's floral scent.

"It's a phase." She cupped his cheeks. "He loves you and knows you love him."

Jim focused on Francesca's gaze as her hands dropped to his chest. "You promise?"

"It's about his own emotions, Jim, not you."

"I was asked today how I could take on someone else's child. I never thought we were shouldering a burden—I felt we were welcoming home a soul who needed us as much as we needed him."

"We did, and we are. We're family, flaws and all."

Six

As soon as the sun was up Saturday morning, Jim and the boys replaced rotted slats on the back fence. Francesca appreciated a well-kept property and Jim was determined to give that to her no matter the season. By eight-thirty, his undershirt was soaked with sweat, Baxter was spending more time playing with his toy boat in a bucket of water, and Ernest was gazing off into the distance rather than passing Jim nails.

"Go on, son," Jim told him.

"Thanks, Jim." Ernest dashed for the house. A minute later, the front screen door snapped behind him when he exited.

Jim pulled off his clinging shirt and tossed it over the laundry line before sticking a few nails between his lips for easy access. He squeezed behind the azalea bushes and hammered in the next slat, imagining the leaves brushing his back were Francesca's fingers.

"I made lemonade," she called.

Jim finished attaching the pine board and maneuvered out of the bushes. Baxter reached his mother first and brought his glass to the table Rochester and Sunny were lounging on.

"Thanks, Fran." Jim took his glass from the tray.

"Do I need to bring you another shirt?"

"It restricts my movement once it's plastered to me, and it's gotta be ninety in the shade." He took a swig of the lemonade.

"Good. I love seeing your glistening skin."

"That's great, seeing as how you get me hot so often."

Francesca laughed and Jim's soul nearly soared to the sky with her pure joy. He leaned in for a kiss. "I love you, baby. I can't wait to dance with you at the party tonight."

"I look forward to unveiling my new dress for you. Bethany Davenport assisted me at the shop."

Francesca had gone downtown the day before, but refused to show Jim what she had purchased at Mademoiselle Bisset's store. The mention of the shop helper made him remember Ernest had his eye on the youngest Davenport. His distraction that morning was probably because he was daydreaming about her.

"Is it short?" Jim asked about the dress.

"Yes, and sleeveless. You'll be able to kiss me anywhere you wouldn't mind doing so in public."

"Then we'll need some private time too." He nipped her neck.

"That's what our hotel room is for—our one-night rendezvous." Francesca's deep brown eyes—full of love and mischief—caused Jim to feel the wonderment of their relationship anew.

"I need to finish the fence so we can leave town."

Two hours later, the fence was complete, Jim was freshly showered, and they dropped Baxter at the Farleys' house. The drive out of town was refreshing with the air blowing through the truck. Francesca sat close to Jim, but they didn't talk. Being together was enough. They stopped at a general store in the town of Theodore for cold colas and boiled peanuts, then made it to the Rolston Hotel in Portersville before the afternoon thunderstorms rolled in off the Gulf.

The three-story hotel was fancy for the bayou, complete with a boathouse equipped with showers for swimmers, plus a pavilion for dancing built right over the water. Their paneled room was cozy, and they showered in the artesian water to get the road dust off before lounging on the bed in their underwear.

"Do you mind if I nap?" Francesca asked as her fingers trailed across his stomach.

"I will if you keep touching me like that." He kissed her forehead and drew her closer.

She stopped her roaming touches and snuggled into the crook of his neck. Jim's jumbled thoughts of Ernest and Baxter threatened to destroy the mood though he knew Deborah would care for the boys as well as she did her own children.

Feeling Francesca's rhythmic breathing against his skin returned Jim's focus to the present. The privacy of the hotel room was a luxury they didn't have in their house. Francesca typically suppressed her passion during their lovemaking so they wouldn't draw the boys' attention amid the shared walls. As soon as she awakened from her nap, Jim planned to bring her to heights worthy of all kinds of noises.

A short while later, heavy rain pattered the windows. Francesca sat up, and Jim immediately fingered across the lace trim of her silk camisole. He kissed her décolletage, noting her stiffening peaks beneath the silk. Then his lips were on her exposed collarbone. Kissing his way down from there, Francesca's sighs turned to gasps. They made love to the sounds of the waning thunderstorm and Francesca's desires, then showered again.

Jim pulled on a white shirt and navy seersucker suit with a red tie, oiled his hair, combed his mustache, and slipped his billfold into a pant pocket, plus his revolver into his jacket as he often did when he wasn't on duty. Then he paced the veranda with a cigarette while Francesca prepared for the evening.

Upon joining him, Francesca gave a slow turn. Jim's grin said all that he couldn't. The royal blue dress barely reached her knees in front but dipped lower in the back. A broad U-neckline displayed her graceful neck, and the thin straps left her delectable shoulders exposed. The silk gown was overlaid with a gauzy netting strung with blue sequins in a vertical stripe pattern. It added height and movement to her willowy frame with the A-line drape of the skirting. And around it all, like a ribbon on a present, was a thin blue belt low on her hips.

Jim dropped his cigarette in a brass receptacle and captured her hands. He kissed her neck, each shoulder, and then in the middle of her upper back before nosing beneath her ear. "I want to devour you all over again, Francesca."

She glowed as she stepped away. "It's Chanel. I'll have to wear it several times to get my money's worth."

"Wear it every day for the rest of your life, if you'd like. You look spectacular. I'm glad you're mine, babydoll—today and always."

Jim proudly escorted Francesca to the hotel dining room. They ate a light dinner of salad and chilled boiled shrimp before going to his pickup. The half a dozen miles were filled with wooded areas along the country roads and fields green from summer rains that blurred past them until Jim slowed.

The mansion that came into view was as impressive as anything designed by George B. Rogers that stood on Government Street. Jim drove around the parking area to get a feel of the property. The house ruled over the cleared land that included a pool pavilion and a plethora of out buildings, plus a bunch of cows and what looked like a dairy an acre beyond the Olympic-sized pool.

Jim parked in the section of the yard near the main road. Arms linked, they crossed the dark field, weaving between parked cars.

Feeling the stares from the two suited men who stood beyond the tiered fountain on either side of the front door of the Mediterranean Revival home, Jim continued toward the bandshell. The five-piece jazz ensemble sounded terrific under the stars as he led Francesca through the throng of moving bodies until he claimed a spot on the edge of the pool area. They started with a fast foxtrot and mixed in a few Charleston moves for variety. Francesca's sparkling dress caught the lights beautifully.

After the second tune, a voice called out. "Hey, Jim!"

Turning, Jim spied Marie Marley. She wore a pink fringed gown every bit as skimpy as Francesca's.

"Hello, Marie." He offered his hand while holding Francesca's with his left. "It's good to see you. I'm sure you remember my wife, Francesca."

"Yes, of course. Shall I show y'all around?" Marie asked.

"I'd rather save that responsibility for Sadie," Francesca replied. "But thank you."

"She doesn't typically come outside until later, but I'll take you to her. Richard wants his hostess to focus on his important guests that tend to stay inside the house."

As they approached the manor, Jim noticed the two guards on either side of the front door allowed some men entrance with a polite bow, but others were patted down. Knowing he'd be in the latter group as a first-time guest, Jim mentally cussed.

The bulky, younger guard cracked a smile at Marie as he tipped his fedora.

"Hey, Orson. This is one of Sadie's oldest friends, Francesca, and her husband, Jim. Sadie will vouch for them being good for the main house."

"We take our orders from Mr. Beauchamp, not the missus," the steely-eyed one said.

"Why don't you check with Sadie and have her announce us?" Jim offered. "We'll be fine out here a bit longer."

"I could bring Francesca in, no trouble. It's only the men Richard is worrisome about." Marie took Francesca's arm. "I'm sure I saw Josephine in here earlier."

The friendly guard opened the door, allowing a refreshing flow of machine-chilled air to escape the house.

"Go on, Fran. Cool off for a bit and say hello. I'll be fine." Jim kissed her, then motioned her inside.

The guard watched after the ladies as they entered. When the door closed, he looked at Jim. "You got yourself a fine woman."

"I know I do." Jim's proud smile lasted as he strolled around the side of the house.

The windows were un-curtained but the panes were closed as the house had air-coolers installed. Gently curved archways rimmed the wide doorways within the wood-trimmed walls that housed a fine collection of art and statuary. A poker game was happening on the side porch, but Jim looped around to the rear double glass doors. It opened to what appeared to be the breakfast room. In the wall beyond, a narrow door opened and a couple walked out of what looked like a small elevator shaft.

Intrigued, Jim's mind mulled over the possibility while he continued to the rose garden. It sat on a rise of earth between the main house and the outbuildings.

Marie stopped at Jim's side. "If you'd like to join your wife, you could go in the house if one of the guards pats you down."

"I wouldn't pass the inspection."

"You naughty thing! You can't bring a weapon into— they'd give you the bum's rush if they knew you were packing heat."

"What's with the guards?"

"They tell Richard everything, no matter how small, though Orson is a sweetheart. Don't worry about Francesca. Sadie already squirreled her away when she escorted Cyrus and Josephine into the space for Richard's choicest guests. I'm afraid you'll never make that final cut, even if your wife gets to tag along with the Harringtons. But don't worry, I'll keep you company. Did you notice the fresh jazz group that's playing? Tabitha Campbell is the pianist. She's the pluckiest thing alive, so unlike her demure mother," Marie prattled. "I can't believe Magdalene Melling is okay with her gallivanting around to parties like this when she's barely of age."

"Tabitha was one of Winnie's first piano students."

"So she was! I'd forgotten. I haven't seen Winnie in months."

"I'm sure she'd enjoy a visit from you."

"It's nauseating to see her bliss over such a modest life when Sean Spunner would have given her the world with proper introductions when she came of age."

"She chose love over all else, which is worthy of respect." Jim motioned to the outbuildings. "Why don't you give me the five-cent tour of the grounds?"

"You already saw the bandshell and pool pavilion." Marie hooked her arm through his as though they were on a Sunday stroll. They descended the few steps toward the back of the property where a couple of smaller houses that matched the architecture and roofing materials of the mansion sat. "These cottages are for the domestics and special guests."

"Are those the garages?" Jim asked, pointing further.

"Yes, and a hanger for an airplane. That belongs to the man Richard acquired things from. I hear he travels stealthily between private properties," she said in a mock whisper.

"The Chicago man?" Jim asked as they continued toward the back fence.

"Yes."

Between the back cottages and the farm beyond was a raised home secluded by a line of trees though Jim could make out the glow of paper lanterns across a balcony. He stopped to study the building. Jazz music spilled from the screened windows as vibrant as the live music at the bandshell.

"What is this place?"

Marie tugged his arm to get him to move. "That's not Richard's, and I'm not supposed to go there. The dairy is beyond it, and the cows spook easily."

"You're a lousy liar, Marie."

"I'm not supposed to go there, and there *are* cows." Marie turned toward the bandshell and resumed their walk, blonde finger waves brushing her cheek as she flashed a coy smile. "I can't believe Fran is wearing Chanel. I wouldn't think a policeman could afford a dress like that for his wife. Are you taking bribes, Jim Abbott?"

"I didn't buy it."

"Don't tell me she has an admirer. Why, she's close to forty, isn't she?"

Jim slowed their pace. "What does her age have to do with anything?"

Marie shrugged, eyes bright with mirth. "Oh, nothing. She's pretty enough, and her figure is trim, but I don't understand her wearing something better than the hostess. It's bad form."

"I don't know about your society's rules, but as far as I'm concerned, Francesca can wear whatever she likes, whenever she wants. She spends her own money when she wants a special dress and I appreciate the results."

"And the boys? Does she often outfit them?"

"I have a modest income, Marie. We aren't in dire straits."

"Her parents were comfortably off, even if they stayed in that little house as a sense of nostalgia. But I don't like seeing all the bungalows going into Washington Square. It brings down the feel of the neighborhood."

"Why shouldn't a family enjoy the comforts of a nice neighborhood in a snug Craftsmen just because their job doesn't give them a fancy office to lounge in during the day?"

"We're worlds apart, aren't we, Jim?" Marie smirked. "Who's watching your sons today, or is Ernest old enough to be in charge?"

"They're at the Farleys' on Rapier."

"The absent-minded math teacher and his spiritualist wife." Marie laughed. "I should have guessed you'd be friends with the neighborhood loonies."

"Does that conclude the tour?" He didn't bother to hide the edge in his voice.

"I suppose it does since I can't get you into the gambling den in the basement. Josephine is lucky Cyrus makes a lot of money designing Mardi Gras tableaux—not to mention his skills with interiors and florals for the grandest homes and celebrations."

"The commissioner can keep his high-class heels. I came here to dance."

"And help me?"

"I already figured things out. That house with the lanterns is a brothel, there's a distillery in the dairy, and all this is orchestrated by Capone."

Marie stopped before they reached the dance area. "His men are all over the property because of his interests on the back acres. Richard is running the casino for him because he can vouch for the local men who want to play. Being a city commissioner, Richard knows everyone with money and who's likely to be undercover when the feds are in town."

"Am I marked? I was on the force when the last two raids went down."

"No offense, but Richard never notices anyone unless they can do something for him." She held his gaze and angled her head in a play of innocence. "Would you ever do anything for him, Jim?"

He scoffed. "Why does Commissioner Beauchamp need his sister-in-law to play middleman?"

"We're old friends, Jim. I wanted to make sure you got the opportunity to accept—"

"You can stop right there, Marie," he said with exasperation. "You and I had some great times together, but that's all it is for me—the past. If you made up that story about fearing what's going on out here in an attempt to sway me to work for rum runners, please know I don't owe you or your family any favors and never will."

"You think you're too good to assist Richard, strutting around because you're the senior member of the Flying Squadron. But don't give yourself airs, Officer Abbott. You're just another man."

"I'm sure any number of men would be flattered with your offer, Marie, but I love my family and don't want them tangled up in anything like this."

"Fine." She minced her way through the crowd.

Jim watched her go with relief. He had no interest in getting caught up with Commissioner Beauchamp or the country's most notorious mobster. Even if helping bring Capone down would give him the career boost he sought, Jim knew how deadly it could be. There was too much he needed to do with safeguarding Ernest to risk anything that big right now.

When Jim made it to the dance floor, he spied Francesca crossing the lawn with Sadie Beauchamp.

"I'm sorry about the misunderstanding at the door," Sadie said as he joined them. "It's good to see you, again, Jim."

"It's no problem, Mrs. Beauchamp."

"Please, call me Sadie. You're welcome in the house on the main floor, but if I were you, I'd not make small talk with anyone about your profession."

"Of course, Sadie." He offered his arm to Francesca. "Are you ready to dance?"

"Yes." Her breath was perfumed with wine.

The next song was one with a Latin beat. Jim stopped before the bandshell. "Let's Argentine Tango, babydoll."

Sharing the slow, provocative movements with Francesca was exhilarating. Cheek to cheek, they were able to exchange heated words while their bodies communed to the beat.

"With or without the new dress, you're the prettiest lady here."

"And you're all I want, Jim." The words caressed his neck with heated passion. "Touch me."

His fingertips trailed her extended arm while they continued the hypnotic footwork. When he'd traveled the length of her smooth skin twice, Jim kissed her shoulder, then her throat. Francesca arched back without missing a step and he kissed his way to the slight swell of her chest.

"Make love to me, Jim."

A whistle and a couple catcalls sounded, but Jim's focus was on his willing wife. He rhythmically bumped against her in an imitation of the ultimate act as they continued to glide through the steps. Then he kissed his way back to her cheek.

"Let's cut out of here soon, Francesca." He nibbled her ear. "We can dance at the hotel and enjoy the waterfront."

"And our bedroom."

"That sounds good too, babydoll, but only if you want—"

"I want you, James Baxter Abbott. Take me back to the hotel after the next dance."

Seven

After supper with the Farleys, Ernest made sure Baxter took a bath and then walked him through the large bedroom Theodore shared with his younger brother. The screened sleeping porch ran the length of the back of the house and was used by all four of the Farley siblings in the summer. Ernest loved being on the second floor and would have happily laid in the breeze, listening to the evening sounds, but he had a goal to accomplish.

"There's your pallet, Bax." Ernest pointed to the bedding closest the door. As the youngest, Baxter was unknowingly the buffer between the two Farley girls on the right side of the porch and Ernest on the left with the boys. Not that Ernest would ever look twice at Eleanor—and surely not the youngest—especially when he had the chance to see Louisa Davenport that night.

"Miss Deborah will come to read to all of us?" Baxter asked as he flopped down on the blankets folded into a makeshift mattress.

"Those who are here. Theo and I are going out, and Eleanor is helping one of her friends roll her hair, so she's down the street right now." Ernest pointed to Theodore's hammock in the corner. "I'll be sleeping over by Theo when we get back. If you need me in the night, just crawl over so you don't trip on anything."

Baxter nodded, eyes wide.

"You've slept here before, lots of times."

"I have?"

"Yeah, but's it's been a couple years. Mom and Dad used to go across the bay for weekends alone every few months. We always stayed with Miss Deborah when they were gone."

"I don't remember."

"You were pretty little."

"Do you think they'll go off like that now that Mommy's feeling better?"

"Probably, but you'll be fine, Bax." He reached over and ruffled his brother's hair. "You're brave like Dad."

Baxter's grin made him look like their father. Ernest leaned down and kissed his forehead because he knew their parents would have if they'd been there. "See you later, Bax."

When Ernest stepped into the bedroom, Deborah was waiting in the doorway to the hall. "He'll be fine, Ernest. You boys have fun."

"Yes, ma'am."

He met her gaze—soft and loving like his mother's, rather than Miss Jo's piercing one. "Remember to harness your power, Ernest. I know it's an important part of you, but you must keep it safe."

He huffed in annoyance. "Jim got to you, didn't he?"

"Your father loves you, Ernest. There's too much potential for wrongdoing if outsiders know of your abilities. I'm called everything from devil woman to witch just as much as Josephine is because I can speak with spirits. If people knew I could also see auras, it would be even worse. As it is, I'm ostracized by the pious and hounded by those desperate to speak to the departed in hopes of discovering the whereabouts of hidden fortunes."

"But you help people."

"I do my best, but if it wasn't for the legitimate concerns of those with a haunted house or the ones mourning a loved one gone too soon, I'd ignore all the pleas. Once Alvin retires from teaching, we'll probably move to the country for a bit of peace."

"There aren't ghosts in the country?"

"Of course there are, but these days I'm more wary of the living," she said with a weary smile. "I don't want to see you being singled out if the public learns of your amazing gift."

"Yes, ma'am."

"I mean what I said about having fun." Deborah squeezed his hand. "Theo thinks he's invincible since he turned sixteen last month, but don't let him get away with too much."

Grinning, he squeezed her hand in return. "Yes, Miss Deborah."

Ernest hurried past her two youngest in the hall and down the stairs to the landing. He paused before the stained-glass window, listening to where Theodore might be. Hearing him say goodbye and hang up the telephone, Ernest turned left to the handful of steps leading into the kitchen rather than the right-side set of stairs that led to the front of the house. He jumped into the room, causing his friend to startle.

"Darn you, Ernie!" Theodore shoved him. "Jack can't go. Do you want to do something else instead? There are plenty of places to get sodas without going all the way to Royal Street."

"I have to get to the Van Antwerp fountain tonight. If you don't come with me, I'll get busted for going alone."

"Oh, all right." Theodore understood that walking alone into the poshest hangout for the high school crowd could be disastrous for guys like them whose fathers weren't in mystic societies nor their mothers on charitable boards. He grabbed several trolley tokens from the drawer of the credenza and looked at the sofa where his father sat beside a lamp, reading a mathematics book. "We're going, Dad."

Mr. Farley looked up, his square face holding a puzzled expression from the interruption.

"Ernie and me, we're going to the soda fountain," Theodore clarified. "Do you want me to let you know when we get home?"

"Your mother will know," he said with a lopsided grin as his eyes returned to the page. "Don't cause any trouble, you hear?"

"Yes, sir."

When Theodore swung open one side of the double front door, Ernest rushed into the night. He was on Government Street before Theodore caught up.

"Now hold up, or I won't give you a token," he told Ernest.

"I'd run there if needed." Ernest raked a hand through his thick hair, smoothing it to the side.

"You got it bad. You should've fallen for a girl that lives closer so you could easily keep track of her. Even if Louisa agrees to go out with you, you won't know if she's stepping out with one of those fancy boyfriends of hers."

"She's not like that, and they aren't boyfriends. Asher and Simon are practically brothers to her. They're kin by marriage—or divorce—or something. They're like cousins, at least."

"Kissing cousins, maybe. I've never seen her without them."

"That's because she's visiting them when she's in the neighborhood, doofus. But when school starts back next month, those guys will be at UMS while Louisa is with us at Mobile High." Ernest glanced at the canopy of oak branches and caused an acorn to drop on Theodore's head.

He rubbed his scalp. "Cut it out, Ernie."

As the streetcar came to a stop, Theodore nudged Ernest's ribs and motioned toward the windows. Several girls he recognized from school were peering out, but he hadn't seen much of them because they were in Theodore's grade. Ernest climbed aboard behind him.

"Good evenings, ladies," Theodore said with a bow before sliding onto the bench across from them.

They giggled, but their smiles fell when Ernest sat next to him. Those two years of seniority were a gulf between kids who remembered what had happened to the Hart family and those who didn't—like that guy in the cemetery. Ernest shifted so he wasn't too close to Theodore, and didn't make eye contact with him or the girls.

"Are y'all headed to a picture show?" Theodore asked.

"Yes," one replied, her smile evident in her perky voice.

Ernest didn't bother to keep paying attention. He knew Theodore was a true pal and wouldn't bail on him when he knew Ernest's goal that night was to ask Louisa Davenport if he could see her in the future.

At the corner of Royal and Dauphin Streets, Ernest and Theodore walked through the doors of the Van Antwerp skyscraper. Inside the gleaming soda fountain room, Ernest perused the space until he saw Louisa in a blue pleated dress on the end seat of a corner booth. Asher and Simon were there, along with Horatio Adams, plus one of Louisa's older half-sisters and a tall man with hair redder than Louisa's.

Spying two open stools near the booth, Ernest led the way through the noisy space, doing his best to walk like Jim did when he climbed off his motorcycle. Confident, a bit of a swagger.

"Don't try too hard," Theodore muttered as they each took a padded stool.

They ordered root beer floats from the soda jerk, then Ernest turned sideways, as though he were sitting that way to better talk with Theodore. It gave him a clear view of Louisa's booth. Her wavy auburn hair curled at the bobbed tips,

outlining her glowing countenance. It was the haircut she'd
returned from her spring trip to Paris with. She looked mature
with her heart-shaped face and high cheekbones. Classy looks
ran in the family because her half-sister looked like she was
twenty instead of sixteen.

Ernest had drunk half his root beer float when Louisa
stood.

"It's okay, Ash," Ernest heard her say over the noise of
the room. "I'm happy to get them."

Body on high alert, Ernest straightened before deciding a
relaxed attitude was best. He watched her approach the
counter out of the corner of his eye and casually turned when
she was a few feet away.

"Hey, Louisa."

"Hi, Ernie." She smiled. "I didn't know you came here."

He lifted a shoulder. "When I have the time. How about
you?"

"At least twice a week. They have the best cola, don't
they?"

"They sure do." Ernest stood, gazing into her brown eyes.

"I need to order two more for Simon and Horatio."

"Sit here while you wait." He tapped his stool.

"You don't mind?"

"Not at all." He nodded to Theodore. "Do you remember
Theo Farley? Theo, this is Louisa Davenport."

"Yes, I think so. Hello." She sat, carefully smoothing her
knee-length skirt and crossing her ankles.

Theodore saluted her and continued spooning out vanilla
ice cream from his glass.

"You'll probably get his father for a math class at some
point in your high school career. He used to teach at Barton,
but moved over to the new high school this past year."

"I hope he's as nice as you, Theo," she said.

Theodore swallowed. "He sure is, Miss Davenport. He coaches the football team as well."

Ernest waved over the soda jerk. "The lady needs two colas for her table, please."

"Thank you, Ernie. What have you been doing this summer? You look like you've been in the sun a lot."

Ernest leaned on the counter and grinned, pleased she'd noticed his tan. "Baseball mostly. I'm going out for the high school team this year, but also some fishing and swimming."

"I swim too. Which club do you go to?"

Theodore laughed, then tried to cover it, which made him snort.

Ernest hooked his thumbs into his pant pockets. "I like a natural setting. Creeks or the bay are best."

"The bay is nicer on the Eastern Shore, but aren't you afraid of alligators and snakes?"

"Nah. I know what signs to look for in regard to dangers."

"Simon is like that too. He was born on Dauphin Island, but Asher doesn't like getting dirty unless it involves the horses. Do you ride?"

"I can't say I've had the opportunity to learn, though I plan on getting a motorcycle once I get a steady job."

"You're brave, Ernie." Her brown eyes shone with wonder.

"Your sodas." The jerk clinked the glasses onto the counter.

Ernest could have kicked him for the interruption.

Louisa thanked the worker and slid him the money before standing.

"I'll get them for you." Ernest followed Louisa, carrying the glasses.

At the booth, Louisa turned to Ernest with a smile to retrieve one. She set it on the table. "Here you are, Simon."

When Simon Campbell saw Ernest, he frowned, but Louisa got between them when she took the next glass.

"And Horatio." She turned back to Ernest. "Thank you for your help."

"Who's your friend?" her sister asked.

"Beth, this is Ernie Abbott. Ernie, my sister, Bethany, and that's her boyfriend, Abe Walker of Dauphin Island. I think you know the others."

"Yeah, because I told him to leave you alone," Simon said, sliding toward the edge of the bench.

"And I told you there's nothing to worry about," Louisa said. "Ernie happened to be sitting at the counter when I went up to order."

"I bet he was eager to help."

"Yes, and he was a perfect gentleman."

As Simon pivoted on the bench to stand, Ernest looked at the nearest glass long enough to tip it in Simon's direction. Cola went down the front of his previously crisp, white shirt.

"Hey!" Simon leapt up as half the room turned toward them. "Why'd you do that, Abbott?"

"He didn't do anything," Louisa snapped. "He wasn't even touching the table."

"He did it, all right." Simon took a stance for a swing at Ernest, but Abe Walker maneuvered his lanky frame out of the booth.

"That's enough, Simon." Abe's freckled hand gripped his ruined shirt by the shoulder. "It was an accidental spill. We all saw there was nothing he could've done to it."

"But he looked at the cola before it happened!"

The manager approached. "Is there a problem here, Mr. Walker?"

"No, just a misunderstanding between the boys."

The manager studied Ernest through his spectacles. "I want you to finish your refreshment and leave quietly."

"Yes, sir." Ernest looked at Louisa and gave her a smile before turning back to the counter.

"Guess your night was a bust," Theodore said after Ernest sat beside him.

"Not at all." Ernest slurped down the rest of his melted root beer float. "I learned Louisa has watched me enough to notice changes, thinks I'm brave, and is willing to defend me against those guys."

"Defend a guilty party," Theodore muttered with a smirk.

"I didn't touch it."

Ernest and Theodore laughed and went to the door. They paused on the sidewalk to decide which route to take home, still grinning. When the door opened behind them, Ernest flinched. A young couple exited and hurried across Dauphin Street after an automobile passed, joining the crowd of pedestrians across the road.

Theodore chuckled and gave Ernest a shove. "Jumpy, ain't ya? Just like a guilty person."

Then Simon and Horatio were there, arms crossed and faces scowling.

"What's going on, fellas?" Theodore asked.

"We're here to teach Abbott a lesson," Simon replied.

"Only two of you?" Ernest noted the trash can behind the boys. "Why didn't your scrawny friend come?"

Simon tightened his fists. "You leave Asher out of this. This is between you and me."

"Then why bring a friend with you?" Ernest briefly glared at Horatio, who had been a grade behind him at Barton Academy.

"Because you've got him." Simon pointed at Theodore, who was several inches taller than all of them. He had the solid build of his father, but preferred to play trumpet and baseball rather than football like Alvin Farley had in his youth.

"I'm man enough to fight you one-on-one if that's what you want." Ernest gave him a deadly stare. "I'm not scared of you, Simon Campbell. Just because you go to a fancy prep school and live in a big house with your stepfather doesn't make you better than me."

"No, but the fact that my father was a war hero rather than a murderer does."

The garbage toppled at Simon's feet, contents from the hot day spilled out along with their putrid odors.

Horatio jumped away, but Simon's shoes were soiled as much as his shirt.

"You're a real heel, Abbott."

"It's not my fault you now smell as rotten as you are." Ernest laughed.

Ernest started walking and Theodore followed. Seconds later, Simon yelped from behind them.

"Are you all right?" a man called as he hurried across Royal Street.

Ernest turned to see Dr. and Mrs. Woodslow join Simon, who was on the sidewalk, holding his arm.

"My foot caught something." Pain was evident in Simon's voice. "I fell and hurt my wrist."

Mrs. Woodslow stopped beside them. "You're Maggie's son, aren't you?"

"Yes, ma'am."

Horatio pointed down the sidewalk at Ernest. "He did it! He pushed him."

Dr. Woodslow squinted in their direction. "Those boys were walking away before he fell. Let me check your arm."

Seeing Mrs. Woodslow watching him while her husband checked Simon spurred Ernest to move.

"Come on," he whispered to Theodore. "Let's catch the next streetcar."

Once they were on Government Street and the hum of the approaching streetcar drowned out their voices, Theodore nudged Ernest.

"That doctor is Judge Spunner's good friend, isn't he?"

"Yeah, so what?" Ernest asked. "We were nowhere near Simon when he fell."

"If the judge knows about you, he might have told his friend. The doctor might put two and two together." Theodore stepped onto the trolley.

"Having a math teacher for a father really messed you up, Theo." Ernest smirked to cover the dread of Jim finding out what he'd done.

Eight

Jim lay in a blissful haze on the hotel bed before dawn. Francesca slept soundly, her skin soft and warm the length of his side where their bodies touched. The gulf wind billowed the sheer curtains, causing Jim to pull the bedsheet up his chest to ward off a chill from the salty air. Curling against him, Francesca's cheek settled above his heart, her left leg and arm draped over him in a way that made him realize he'd never be complete without her. He gently stroked her hair as he marveled at the feeling of absolute connection to the moment—to his wife. Physically, their bodies had communed for hours in a splendid passion from the dancefloor to the bed. The sensual joining continued on a spiritual level when he manifested his love through each beat of his heart as they held each other in the dark.

He reached the sheet to cover her bare shoulders. Francesca shifted closer, a leg wrapping his with a hooking motion of her foot under his knee.

"I'm yours, baby." He enveloped her completely while his kisses slowly roamed.

By the time the rosy glow of sunrise met the stretch of lawn that reached to the gulf in front of the Rolston Hotel, Jim and Francesca were wrapped together in a blanket on the floor beneath the open window.

"It's beautiful," she said as Jim held her. "I've never seen those colors before."

"It reminds me of your blush of climax," he whispered as his hand trailed from the crown of her head to her graceful neck.

"My flush of pleasure and your burning heat as you fuse your aura to mine."

He nodded and kissed her brow, then her jaw. "This night has meant everything to me, Francesca."

"It's been magical, Jim."

"Thank you for healing and balancing me with your love and through what we've shared." Jim lifted her to the bed, laying with her at the foot of it so they could see the expanse of daybreak over the water. "I hope to remember this moment for the rest of my life."

That afternoon, Jim knocked on the Farleys' door before looking back at Francesca sitting in his truck at the curb. Her broad smile was visible even as the sky darkened with an approaching thunderstorm. The front door opened, turning Jim's attention.

"Your aura is marvelous!" Deborah said as she took his hand. "I've never seen it so crisp."

"I feel more grounded than ever."

"And you look it. How was the party, Jim?"

"Terrific. How were the boys?"

"Just fine. Baxter is in the garden, and Ernest is out with Theodore. I'll tell him you're back when they return." Deborah studied him a moment longer. "There's a hint of Fran in your aura. Be sure you don't take too much from her when you connect."

Jim shrunk with the news, dropping her hand. "I ta—I didn't realize! Is she harmed?"

"Sometimes you give and sometimes you take. I doubt Fran is any worse from the connection, but I'll check her. The boys' things are inside the door."

Wanting to be sure of Francesca's well-being made him hesitate on the threshold.

"Go on, Jim," Deborah said. "I'll see you at the truck."

Down the hall beyond the dining room, Jim passed through the tidy kitchen and exited the back porch.

"Hey, Bax!"

Baxter jumped up from under a rose bush, where he was corralling a toad with the youngest Farley and ran the short gravel path that crunched beneath his boots. "Daddy!"

Jim lifted him and kissed his cheek. "Have a good time, son?"

"Yes! What about you and Mommy?"

"It was marvelous, but we missed you and Ernest." Jim set him back on his feet and ruffled his hair. "Say goodbye, and then we'll get home."

At the truck, Jim tossed the boys' bags into the back beside his and Francesca's as Baxter climbed onto Francesca's lap. Deborah said farewell to both, closed the truck door, and joined Jim at the rear of the vehicle.

"She's as clear and bright as you are," Deborah informed him. "And she has a notable amount of you in her aura. Your activities did you both well."

Jim blushed under the innuendo.

"She's a great source of strength for you, Jim. If you want to focus on your connection and return to your quarterly getaways, please know I'm happy to host the boys anytime."

"Thanks, Deborah." He gave her a quick hug. "I know Fran loves autumn on the Eastern Shore."

Thunder rumbled as he got behind the wheel. At home, Jim carried the luggage inside before rain pattered against the roof. Francesca set water on the stove to prepare tea while she unpacked, allowing Jim time with Baxter. After seeing his son yawn twice while he read to him from a Rudyard Kipling story, Jim closed the book.

"I think you need a short nap, Bax. Rest up and then we can play more before dinner."

"All right."

Jim kissed his forehead, then paused to study the green eyes peering up at him. "I love you, son."

"Love you too, Daddy. I was nervous about staying overnight away from home, but Ernest helped me."

"He's a great big brother. I'm glad you have each other."

Jim concentrated on radiating his love as Baxter relaxed into his pillow. He reluctantly admitted to himself that Jo was right in telling him to utilize his abilities. The feeling of peace that enveloped him when he expanded his aura was met with returning warmth at the feel of Francesca's relaxation against him and the sight of his son smiling as he drifted to sleep.

A knock rapped at the front door as Jim closed Baxter's bedroom. Francesca reached the entry first. Judge Spunner stood on the porch. His blue summer suit was spattered with rain drops, and he held his wet hat, head of graying hair on full display.

"Sean, what a surprise!" Francesca opened the screen door. "To what do we owe the honor of a visit from Mobile's favorite judge?"

"Thank you for the welcome, darling." He kissed her cheek and looked her over, leering appreciatively. "It's been much too long."

"You're a lecherous old coot," Jim said with false gruffness.

The judge flashed his impish smile. "Hello, Jim."

"Come in and have a seat," Francesca said as she hung his hat and took the judge's suit jacket. "How's Hattie?"

"Glorious and as lively as ever. She does miss sparring with Jo at her science clubs though. I practically begged her to rejoin. Jo did say if she couldn't goad me, my wife is the next best option."

"That sounds like her. And your children, are they well? On our visits to Jo's, Clive sometimes mentions Brandon when talking about school."

"They're wonderful. Althea keeps us all in line."

"Good. You need it."

"I believe you've been around Josephine too much. You seem to have caught her snark." The judge turned his attention to Jim. "And how's the city's best officer of the peace?"

"I'm well, thank you. Would you care for a drink? We're just back in town, but I'm sure there's—"

He waved his hand in dismissal. "I'm fine, thank you. I just finished a late luncheon with my family. Are the boys home?"

"Ernest is out with Theo Farley, and Baxter is napping."

"Good. I need to tell you what I heard on the cathedral portico after Mass."

Francesca smiled. "What naughty bit of gossip is spreading this weekend that's too scandalous for young ears?"

Judge Spunner took a deep breath. "It's not naughty in the way you imply, but I overheard Grace Anne talking with her mother. Apparently when she and John were leaving the Trellis Room last night they saw several boys outside the Van Antwerp building. A trash can fell over, upsetting one of them. It turned out to be Simon, Alex Melling's youngest stepson. Thinking it looked like trouble, Grace Anne encouraged John to check on them. On their way over, a couple boys walked away and the other two—Simon and a friend—turned to go inside. Simon tripped, breaking his wrist in the fall. Fortunately, John was able to cast it right away."

"That's too bad for the Melling boy, though he's lucky a doctor was there," Francesca said. "But it isn't exactly gossip-worthy."

"The two boys that walked away were Ernest and Theo. According to Simon and his friend, Ernest is responsible for tripping him, as well as spilling cola on him inside and making the trash receptacle fall at his feet. No witnesses to any event could see how Ernest was to blame because he wasn't within touching distance." The judge paused. "But I think we all know how he did it."

Jim rubbed a hand over his stubbly jaw. "I knew the day was coming."

"Is everyone talking about Ernest?" Francesca asked.

"No, John asked me privately about him. He remembers some of my questions about institutions back when you were going through custody talks, and we weren't sure how Ernest would handle everything. I never mentioned names, but with the Hart family's situation all over the newspapers back then, John guessed who the boy was."

"We never asked you to look into institutions," Jim said pointedly.

"I like to be prepared for anything, and you had me ready to defend him, should it be needed. I never confirmed it was Ernest, but after what he saw and heard last night, the good doctor is convinced your son is more than he appears to be."

"But his wife and mother-in-law are the biggest gossips in town!" Francesca's voice rose in alarm.

"True," the judge said as he patted her knee, "but Grace Anne didn't see Ernest do anything, and only John knows that Ernest might possess some otherworldly abilities. Mrs. Marley and Grace Anne are more interested in what was happening between the young people inside Van Antwerp's than complaints about physical upsets."

"And what was that?" Francesca asked.

"Ernest being threatened by Simon to keep away from Louisa Davenport. Abe Walker had to step in to prevent Simon from striking Ernest."

"I've known Abe since he was running the decks of his father's boat," Jim said. "He was a freckled hellion at the wharves whenever they came in from the island. I'd heard he's on track to make captain, but haven't crossed paths with him for a couple years."

"He's all grown up, but still has a rascally glint in his eye, even with Bethany Davenport on his arm."

"Abe Walker is dating a Davenport?" Jim laughed despite his grievances over the situation. "There might be hope for Ernest yet."

"I just saw Bethany last week when I bought my new dress."

"You in a Mademoiselle Bisset gown is always enchanting," the judge remarked with a flirtatious smile to lighten the mood.

"I wore it to Sadie and Richard's party last night."

"Pity you weren't at the one I attended a few weeks ago. Perhaps a kiss from you would have brought me better luck at the tables."

"Don't go back there," Jim said.

"I can afford to lose a little here and there. Hattie wasn't even annoyed, and John and Grace Anne expect us to go whenever they do."

Jim held the judge's stare so he could see how serious he was. "Don't go back, and keep everyone you love away from that property."

Judge Spunner raised his brow. "Is it cursed?"

"In a manner of speaking, but I insist on this, Judge Spunner. You don't want to be wrapped up with what's going on there."

"Then I should host a glamorous party of my own some weekend so I can see Francesca's new dress." He stood, then leaned over her hand to kiss the back of it. "It was wonderful to see you, darling, though I apologize for the bad news."

"Thank you for continuing to look after Ernest."

Jim stood to see him out.

With Judge Spunner gone, Jim collected his truck keys. Francesca met him in the hall.

"I'm going to visit Miss Eilands. I'll be back in about an hour."

"I don't have anything to send her this time," Francesca remarked.

"If my plan works out, you can send something her way tomorrow and every day this week." He kissed her in parting.

Jim drove toward the river, allowing the post-storm freshness to clear his head before the returning heat caused the city to steam. It was the last day of July, but there was still August to get through—the worst for weather and often for criminal activity too.

After parking his pickup, he made his way through the muddy yard, accompanied by a dozen felines and a couple of dogs.

"Afternoon, Miss Eilands!" He called through the screen door.

"Jimmy?" her feeble voice replied. "You can come in."

She was resting in the thread-bare armchair in the dusty parlor, feet on a pile of yellowing newspapers and cats perched on every surface in the room.

"I hope you didn't bring me a pile of things to cook," she remarked as Jim carried over a little stool from the corner to sit on beside her.

"I'm empty-handed today."

She sighed with relief. "Some do-gooders from the parish brought me potato salad at noon. That stuff sits like a rock in my belly. I've been here ever since."

"A great lady like you laid up by potatoes?"

"Potatoes are for winter and famine—not summer." Miss Eilands smiled, wrinkling her shriveled face more. "Where's that wife of yours, Jimmy? It feels like you're carrying a piece of her though I haven't seen her in weeks."

"She's always in my heart and doing very well right now. Francesca and the boys have been spending several days a week out in Spring Hill this summer, and we recently returned from an overnight trip to the South County, just the two of us."

Nodding, her mouth twitched as though to smile. "I can tell you're closer than ever, but what of the trouble with the little mister? I know that's why you're here."

"Judge Spunner dropped by last hour and—"

Miss Eilands straightened, grabbing Jim's hand with her cold, dry one. "Did he have a vision?"

"A vision?" Puzzlement drew his brows together. "The judge?"

The old lady relaxed back into the chair. "Sean Spunner is as much an Irish witch as I am, Jimmy. He's a cunning one—always pretending to be innocently fascinated about others' gifts while safeguarding his own."

"How do you know about it?"

"Like you, he spent his earliest years around these parts. He played the craftiest tricks in his youth and the biggest were on his friends. He'd pretend to be captured by me and spin some yarn to the other boys about narrowly escaping when he'd been enjoying a cup of tea the whole hour. Young Spunner told me about his dreams of death and wanted to know if he could change the outcomes of them."

"Dreams?"

"He dreams of people before they die." Miss Eilands patted Jim's hand, then withdrew her cool, papery touch so she could cross her arms as though seeking to warm herself. "Not everyone, but those close to him, like his granny, parents, and lovers."

"If it's about family, why were you worried when I told you he dropped by?"

"Those he holds dear, Jimmy. His most recent vision was Frederick Davenport. He urged him to go to the doctor last autumn, but the man refused."

"The judge knew Major Davenport had cancer?"

"Sean Spunner didn't know what illness would take the man, just that he would waste away. Seeing it in his dream was enough to keep him from visiting him during his final months—he couldn't bear to see a once mighty man reduced to skin and bones."

"But why hasn't he told anyone?"

Miss Eilands smiled. "A man like him guards his perceived weaknesses. I know, and he's admitted to crying with his wife over his dreams. I think he might have told a few others about it, but keep the trust, Jimmy."

"Yes, ma'am."

"Now what of the little mister?"

"Ernest is testing his limits and making dangerous choices to humble those who try to keep him down. He might have had too much freedom this summer, but I want to reign him in a bit by having him attend to your needs this week. Work, rather than play. Give him a chance to be of service to someone."

"I won't be punishment for him, Jimmy."

"Not punishment, Miss Eilands. More like refocusing." Jim noticed her milky blue eyes were cloudier than ever and wondered how much physical vision she still had. "Put him to work around here so he's engaged in honest labor rather than goofing around with friends or showing off for girls."

"Would that have worked for you?" she countered.

"Maybe for a few days, but I would have appreciated the experience long afterwards."

✳✳✳

When Ernest arrived home at five-thirty, Jim stood from the rug in the parlor where he'd been fixing Baxter's toy fire engine.

"There you go, Bax. I'll be back in a few minutes."

Jim followed Ernest to his bedroom.

"Welcome home, son."

"Thanks." Ernest sat on the edge of his bed and removed his shoes. "Did you have a good time on your trip?"

"I did, but we came home to some startling news."

His blue eyes—looking pale against his tanned face—held Jim's gaze as he straightened.

"Judge Spunner came by a few hours ago and told us what you did at the Van Antwerp building last night." Jim paused to see if Ernest would defend himself, but he didn't. "You've been told by multiple people what you aren't supposed to do outside these walls. Obviously you need something concrete to help you remember. Starting now, you're not allowed to leave the house unless you're attended by your mother or myself. And beginning tomorrow morning, I'll escort you to and pick you up from Miss Eilands, who you're going to be of service to every day this week."

Ernest's shoulders drooped.

"Miss Eilands is nearly blind and isn't getting around well. You can clean, cook, and whatever else she needs help with. I'm hoping some time away from games will remind you what's important in life."

"My power is important!"

"Safeguarding it is vital!" Jim returned.

Ernest sat back on the bed. "No one saw me do anything."

"People aren't stupid. There can't keep being accidents around you, especially happening to your enemies. Simon and his friend think you did those things, and Dr. Woodslow is figuring it out. Not to mention Simon breaking a wrist is assault. No son of mine is going to bully others!"

"His wrist broke?" Panic filled his voice. "I didn't mean for that to happen, Jim. I wasn't even looking at him when I sent a tremor through the sidewalk."

Clinging to the hope Ernest's declaration brought, Jim softened his voice. "I know you're just trying to figure yourself out while making way with the Davenport girl, but you need to hold to reason before you get yourself in a bind I can't help you out of."

"I'm learning there's nothing I can't protect myself from. Just the other week, I was outnumbered three to one and managed to spook the older boys in the cemetery. They ran away in fear."

"Yourself, maybe, but don't forget about your family and friends." Jim dropped his voice, but the emotion rang clear. "Others might not catch you, but what do you think they'd do to the friend or little brother of someone they think is using devilry?"

Understanding washed over Ernest's face. "Miss Deborah said she's called satanic because she talks to spirits and Miss Jo, too, because people think she's a witch."

"And who do you think would get a visit from the vengeful if there's mania against evil Mobile?" Jim placed a hand on his shoulder. "Don't lash out over petty things, son. Save it for when it matters most."

Ernest shrugged off his touch.

Giving him space, Jim left the room. The door immediately closed behind him.

Nine

Jim drove his truck in the morning so he could take Ernest to Miss Eilands's on his way to work. He said goodbye and watched Ernest walk through the bleak yard and into the dilapidated house with the basket of baked goods from Francesca, glad to see his bearing wasn't defeated.

"Keep him safe, Miss Eilands," Jim muttered. "If you can't get him to see sense, no one can."

During roll call and the morning briefing, Jim sat beside Officer Murphy. Highlights for the month of August were noted, including the annual "Buyers' Week" that started the following Tuesday, which gave all the Traffic Officers headaches because of the extra assignments during the worst month of the year. But the next topic change didn't prove to be a welcome one, either.

"There's been a slowdown with the juvenile criminal activities since the patrols have increased," the lieutenant said, "but the brawls are going on at all hours of the day, which is a typical summertime issue because the boys are bored without school. They like to congregate around fields. Try to engage them in a ball game or something if you see a bunch out together. And as for traffic duties, Abbott, you're on the causeway today. Circle back to the south when you can, but the traffic has been heavy along the bay, and people get impatient when waiting for the boats to pass under the draw bridge."

"Good luck out there," Officer Murphy told Jim after the meeting was dismissed. "I did the causeway several times in the past month. There's not a lick of shade during the day, and the nights are eerily quiet."

Jim nodded and donned his hat. "I'll survive. How are your girls, Happy?"

"The sweetest, prettiest things in town. The youngest is looking more like her mother every day." He grinned. "How was the trip with your wife?"

"Terrific. I wish we could have stayed in Portersville a couple more days."

"Careful, Abbott, or you'll end up with another one on the way."

"Naw, we're done on that end of things. I've got my hands full as it is. You're lucky you've got all girls."

"Trouble with the oldest?" Officer Murphy asked as they exited the back door.

"I've got him on restriction this week."

"Good luck with that." He clapped Jim's shoulder and smiled.

They parted ways in the yard. Jim waited for Officer Murphy to drive out first, then he left the congestion of the city behind. The sight of the water reflecting the blue sky beyond the low strip of land surrounded by the river delta created the urge for Jim to grab a fishing pole. Brackish water in his nostrils as the wind swept his cheeks made the yearning even stronger.

The vertical lift was up on the center section of Cochrane Bridge, allowing a river boat to steam north between the four other metal sections. The line of waiting automobiles was already a couple dozen deep. Jim slowly passed the cars in the opposite lane that was clear of oncoming traffic as he daydreamed about leaving town. What he wouldn't give to escape to the Eastern Shore with Francesca for a few days— sooner rather than later.

He rode to the raised section of the bridge and turned around. Facing the drivers and their passengers, Jim assessed each face he passed as he slowly drove west. A few familiar Mobilians escaping the heat of the city were inter-mixed with summer travelers. He inclined his head to the adults and lifted a hand in greeting whenever he saw a kid.

"Hey, officer!" a middle-aged driver hollered, then honked his horn.

Jim pulled to a stop beside the coupe.

"When's this damn bridge going to lower? I've got a meeting in Daphne to get to!"

"It should be functional in about fifteen more minutes, sir," Jim replied as he set his kickstand.

"Get a move on!" the man shouted toward the raised trestle and laid on his horn twice more.

"Sir, I need you to stop using your horn. Everyone can see there's nowhere to go. It doesn't help the situation to agitate people."

"But it helps me feel better."

The horn blared for ten solid seconds while Jim climbed off his bike. Once both feet were on the asphalt, he paused to expel a healing breath so he wouldn't mirror the driver's emotional state when he approached the hothead.

"Sir," Jim said as he stood by the driver's door, "I'd hate to double charge you with disorderly conduct and excessive noise when you have an important meeting to attend. There's not much longer to wait, and it would surely be more uncomfortable for you to stand around in the sun with handcuffs on while we wait for the transport wagon to pick you up."

The driver grumbled something Jim was glad he didn't understand and looked south toward the bay to signal he was done with the conversation.

Jim returned to his motorcycle, sighed in relief, and continued down the row.

A luxury vehicle pulled to a stop at the end of the line. The driver leaned over the door of the open-topped car and waved Jim over as he approached. Jim circled the Lincoln Touring automobile with Texas plates, admiring the lines of the sleek green car rather than the four women inside it. He parked on the shoulder of the road and dismounted. Hurried whispers from the three brunettes and blonde as he approached the passenger side brushed the ill feelings of his previous stop aside.

"Good morning, ladies."

"Hey there, officer," the driver said with a slight drawl as she adjusted her cloche hat.

"Is there anything I could help y'all with?"

"How long is this backup going to be? We're trying to reach Pensacola Beach by noon."

"The bridge will be ready for automobiles within ten minutes, and Pensacola Beach is about two and a half hours down the road. I'd say y'all will be fine."

"Thank you, officer," the driver replied. "I sure wish they were as nice as you in Mississippi. We had a flat tire along Biloxi Beach yesterday, and the policeman there wanted to ticket us for being double parked. While we were in Biloxi, we read up about those flogging trials over here."

"That's up north a good piece, not in Mobile."

"So you don't have trouble with masked men running around to inflict pain?" the driver countered.

Jim crossed his arms, searching for a way to lighten the dreaded topic of the Klan. "Maybe come Mardi Gras, though the revelers are liable to be wielding gilded pigs' bladders rather than whips. Folly chases Death instead of seeking to bring it."

He smiled over their obvious bewilderment of Mobile's Mardi Gras traditions before they laughed in return.

"Well," Jim said as he lifted his cap and took a step back, "y'all have fun on your adventure and get home safely."

Jim straddled his motorcycle and started the engine. He drove the length of the traffic line once more, offering a wave to the ladies when he passed them on his way to the new end of the line. Once the automobiles were moving in both directions, he drove back into town to patrol his other area.

Outside a little corner store, there were half a dozen teens leaning against the weathered wall. The one with a headful of black curls rapped a large stick against the wood building with a menacing beat.

Pleased to finally get a look at the supposed leader of the group, Jim pulled up next to the sidewalk. "How's it going fellas?"

The curly-haired one set his glare on Jim. Though a year or two older than most in the group, he was much too young to have such hardness in his eyes. "We ain't doin' nothin' wrong, officer."

"I didn't say you were, though the owner of the store might not enjoy that drumming no matter how steady your rhythm is."

The young man swung the stick around and began to clap it against his palm while staring at Jim. To show he wasn't intimidated, Jim got off his bike and approached the boys. He hoped to get them talking so they'd share information without it looking like he was interrogating them.

"What do y'all do to stay cool in this weather?" Jim asked.

"We swim at the club and have root beer floats at Van Antwerp's," the leader said, causing the others to laugh.

"More like skinny dipping in the nearest creek and scrounging the alleys for empty bottles to turn in for recycling money so you can get an extra cola." Jim grinned when a few of them looked surprised. "I grew up not too far from here. I know what it's like come summer."

"Yeah, so what are you doing in that uniform, working for the city idiots?" the eldest asked.

"Serving in the Army during the war knocked some sense into me. I wanted to help the community be a safer place. The war straightened me out, but it doesn't have to take trench warfare to make a fella see what's important."

The heftiest boy nodded to the curly-haired leader. "Ryan's dad died in the war."

"Shut your trap or I'll shut it for ya!" Ryan jumped toward him, brandishing the stick.

Jim snatched it from him with his gloved hand.

"Hey!"

"Hey yourself, Ryan. My name's Officer Abbott." He waited a few seconds before offering the stick back to him. "War has a way of changing a fella, both the ones on the front and the ones at home."

Ryan grabbed it and moved to the corner of the building.

Jim turned his attention to the others, but kept Ryan in his peripheral vision in case he made an aggressive move. "What are all your names?"

"Scotty." The pudgy boy crossed his arms in front of his protruding belly as though he didn't mind that Ryan had almost clobbered him.

He'd be the one to work with, but Jim took a minute for introductions from the other four.

"Y'all know any of the officers who walk the beat over here?"

"We tend to hightail it when we see one of them," Scotty said.

"Give Officer Keegan a try next time you see him. He's the one who likes to whistle when he's walking. He's been around longer than me and has a lot of stories to tell if you ever want to ask him anything."

"Why would we want to talk to a cop?"

Jim shrugged and strolled towards his bike. "I thought you might be interested in finding out we're regular fellas. I'll see y'all later."

"Not if I can help it," Ryan spat.

Jim revved the engine and did a circle in the middle of the road before heading back to the causeway for more glaring sun and potentially hostile tourists.

***

Jim parked his pickup outside the gate at Miss Eilands's house and sat for a moment. Barking, squeals of children, and a woman's nagging tirade filled the neighborhood. Shaking his head at the lack of peace after a long patrol day, he walked through the yard, trying to avoid the cats who rubbed against his boots.

"Come on now, I just want to get my boy and go home," he said with exasperation as he tripped his way to the stoop. "Good evening, Miss Eilands!"

Not waiting for a welcome, Jim opened the screen door. A couple cats ran in before he could block their path, but the old lady wouldn't mind. The tile on the kitchen floor was free of dirt, the counters mostly clean. He followed the cleared—but not polished—wood floor down the dark hall to the parlor. Miss Eilands sat in the rocking chair amid a straightened sitting room, a white and black feline on her lap and a smile on her wrinkled face.

"Hello, Jimmy. The little mister worked himself good today, hasn't he?"

Jim took in the stacks of newspapers along the side wall, knowing she'd never part with them, but Ernest had done the best he could. For the first time in the past five years, Jim could take a seat in the chair beside hers.

"He sure did. Where is he?"

"I gave him a break last hour since he did so much, but haven't seen him since."

"That's not what you agreed to," Jim said.

"I didn't agree to anything, Jimmy." She pushed up on the armrests to stand and seemed to look down at him with her milky eyes. "You came here yesterday and told me the little mister would be coming all week without asking me if it would be troublesome, so don't fuss at me for keeping charge of my own house. If you expect him here five days in a row, and he's going to work himself into a frenzy each of those days, I'll be pulling hair come Thursday to find something to occupy him."

"Fair enough," Jim said in resignation. "But where did he go, and when did you tell him to be back?"

"I have no idea where he went, but I told him he better return before you did because he'd get us in trouble. Not that I'd worry a stitch if you're upset with me."

"I'm sorry I'm late, Miss Eilands," Ernest said from the doorway. His hair was darkened with sweat, forehead glistening.

Jim stood and crossed his arms over his uniform. "You didn't take into consideration that this house is a heap closer to the station than ours, did you?"

"No, sir."

"Where'd you go, son?"

"Van Antwerp's for a cola."

"Looking like that?"

"I dusted off a bit." Ernest looked down at his sweat-stained clothes. "I got wetter on the way back because I was running. But Louisa wasn't there so it didn't matter what I looked like."

Jim shook his head. "It'll matter to your mother if she finds out you were in town without wearing for-good clothes."

"You're gonna tell her?"

"Your work for Miss Eilands is between the three of us. But next time, take your break here."

Ernest sighed. "Yes, sir."

"Do you need anything before we go, Miss Eilands?"

"No, Jimmy. Thank you for bringing the little mister. And tell Fran the biscuits were delicious."

"I will, ma'am. We'll see you tomorrow."

Ernest was quiet in the truck. When they crossed Broad Street, Jim broke the silence.

"You did great work today, Ernest. I haven't seen the kitchen and parlor that tidy in years, and more importantly, Miss Eilands looked happy. Your company did her good."

Ernest shrugged. "I'm just doing what you told me."

"You can still be pleased about a job well done."

"I guess." Ernest leaned his arm on the passenger door so he could stick his head out the side of the truck.

When Jim pulled into the yard, Baxter ran down the porch steps and straight over to Ernest.

"How was the cat lady?" Baxter asked.

"She's fine." Ernest put an arm around Baxter and they walked to the house together. "What did you do today?"

"Mommy brought me…" his voice trailed off as they went inside.

Jim smiled over their brotherly affection as he went through the backyard to the screened porch. Pulling out a chair at the old dinette table, he removed his boots and holster.

"I'm home," he hollered while he disrobed.

"I'm prepping a few things for supper, but will be done in a minute," Francesca called through the kitchen door.

When he was down to his undershirt and riding pants, he took a cigarette and perched on the picnic table, bare feet on the plank bench. Sunny jumped up next to Jim and collected a few rubs before sprawling a foot away because even for the cat it was too hot to sit on his lap.

Jim was down to the last inch and a half of his Lucky Strike when Francesca came out. The pink dress she wore billowed about her knees as she walked across the lawn. Her hair was pulled back with combs decorated with freshwater pearls which showcased the small streaks of gray at her temples.

"Hey, babydoll." He spoke around his smoke so he could use both hands to tug her by the hips until she was nestled between his knees. Keeping hold of her buttocks with one hand, he removed the cigarette with his other so he could kiss her.

Francesca leaned into the connection before reaching for the smoldering cigarette Jim let her take. A few years back, she had started finishing his cigarettes when she happened upon him with a little left. She never accepted her own and always blushed when she smoked, dogged by her mother's words that "real ladies didn't smoke," but that made her even more alluring.

She exhaled as Jim's hands trailed her waist. "How was your day, Jim?"

"Long and hot. I had causeway patrol, among my other duties. Tourists were out in force and the town people cranky. How about you?"

"Baxter was clingy. I had to make up games to keep him occupied. Though Ernest is typically gone with his friends, he knew his brother was at Miss Eilands's and thought he should be there too."

"I don't want you and Bax over there because you'd help with the work Ernest needs to do himself. Why don't you see if Winnie would like a visit sometime this week? I'm sure playtime with her kids would improve Baxter's mood."

"I thought of that earlier, but with Arabella, though I don't want to go to Jo's without Ernest being able to." She took another drag.

"Winnie makes more sense right now."

Francesca's eyes narrowed as she leaned over to tap out the cigarette in the ashtray. "Winnie is sweet, but since I knew her mother first, I'm always reminded that she's a decade younger than me, even if she has kids Baxter's age. And you know Jo's my best friend."

"But Winnie's just a couple blocks away. You wouldn't have to bother with the streetcars."

She huffed. "You've got an excuse for everything."

"I prefer to think of it as logic."

"I bet you do."

"Fran, baby, I was trying to be helpful. Go wherever you'd like." Jim put his arms around her. "I'll drive you to Jo's first thing in the morning if needs be."

"Thanks, Jim. I'll think about it."

She kissed his cheek and hugged him in return while he relished the feel of their bodies wrapped together in the twilight.

Ten

After supper, Ernest got permission to listen to the Will Rogers radio program with Jack across the street. Mr. and Mrs. Reardon sat in their armchairs. She was mending the knee of one of Jack's trousers, and he was bent over a broken wristwatch.

Ernest and Jack sprawled on the rug in front of the radio cabinet. It was blissful to lay there without Jim watching his every move or a dozen cats climbing on him as they had when Ernest took a break at Miss Eilands's house. But Ernest didn't want to laze around when he had a lot to accomplish. Even with the progress at the soda fountain Saturday night, Louisa was still out of his reach.

"I'm gonna go," Ernest whispered. "Don't make a deal out of it. Maybe I can leave without your parents noticing in case Jim asks them about me being here."

Jack leaned closer. "Where ya goin'?"

"To see if Louisa is at the Mellings' house."

Ernest slowly sat. When neither adult glanced over, he stood and crept toward the kitchen. He let himself out the back, glad Jack's older brother wasn't home that evening because Tommy would want to know Ernest's every move.

In case someone at home was looking outside, Ernest walked toward Palmetto Street so he could say he was going to the park if needed. But instead of turning left, he went right.

When he reached Roper Street, a voice called out. "Good evening, Ernest."

Feeling caught, he flinched before taking a few steps toward one of the two-story houses that were the foundation of the neighborhood. He tried to discern the details of the woman sitting on the front porch steps because there were typically a lot of ladies at the Marleys house. "Yes, ma'am."

"Come here a moment, won't you? I haven't gotten a good look at you in years."

Ernest used the front walk rather than cut across the lawn. The porch light showcased pale, wavy bobbed hair. Surprised at her prettiness, he smiled when he stood before the woman.

"Why, you're practically a man now, Ernest." She offered an embossed cigarette case. "Smoke?"

"Yes, thank you."

He took one from the silver case and nonchalantly put it between his lips like he'd seen Jim do hundreds of times. She flicked a lighter and extended her arm. Glad that he'd practiced how to smoke properly with Tommy and Jack, he didn't cough with his first puff or even his third.

"It's good quality, ma'am."

Her own cigarette looked graceful between her slim fingers. "Much better than what Jim Abbott uses, I'll bet."

Ernest gave a quick nod and shrugged, unsure how to respond. "I'm sorry, but I don't remember your name."

"I'm Marie Marley, a friend of Jim's."

"Not Miss Fran?"

"Francesca is friends with one of my older sisters, Sadie Beauchamp."

"They went to a party at the Beauchamps' over the weekend."

"Yes, I saw them there. I've been friends with Winnie Paterson since high school. I met Jim when he lived in the apartment above her."

"Jim was living there when I met him too."

Marie exhaled a tight circle of smoke and smiled. "And now Nathan Paterson is on the radio with his news program, and Jim is the lead motorcycle officer for the police. Did you hear Nathan's evening report about the trouble with youth in Mobile this summer?"

"No, Miss Marley." He shifted his weight, unsure if he should stand closer.

"Call me Marie." She moved over on the steps. "And please sit down. It'll be easier to talk, and you don't seem like a troublesome youth, so I'm sure I'll be safe."

Ernest settled a foot away. "I try not to be, but sometimes I think Jim sees me as one."

"But you're so mature, Ernest."

"Not to him, and call me Ernie. All my friends do. I don't think Jim remembers what it's like to be young." He fiddled with the cigarette, accidentally causing some ash to fall onto his pants, which he hastily brushed off.

"On the contrary. I believe Jim remembers exactly what it's like to be on the cusp of manhood and wants to make sure you don't make the same choices he did." She put out her cigarette on the step before flicking it into the flowerbed and leaning closer. "But even with the things he did, he turned out all right, didn't he?"

Ernest nodded, his long bangs falling over his right eye.

Marie quickly brushed it back. "How many girls is a handsome guy like you stringing along?"

"None, Miss—Marie." He felt his face heat.

"You've got your eye on one, I bet."

"Yes, ma'am, but my friends think she's out of my league. She's a society girl with a big house, fancy friends, and a stamped passport. She even went to private school up until now."

"You converse beautifully, Ernie, and manners are important."

"She has remarked on them, but it's not everything."

"No, not everything." Marie pursed her lips when she paused. "I bet you want to use magnetism."

"Yes, exactly." Ernest smiled at her understanding.

"Well, you've got a great start. Girls tend to like a man with touchable hair and your eyes have the quality to be piercing. And you look like you're strong."

"But how do I showcase all these things?"

"There are a thousand ways to do that, Ernie. I don't know where to begin."

"But you're the first one to understand my dilemma. Could you coach me in how to win a society girl?"

Marie lifted her shoulder noncommittally. "What would your parents think?"

"Jim and Fran don't need to know, and I'm a quick learner. Miss Jo has…" Ernest's voice trailed off. He tried to cover the stumbling by putting out the cigarette against the porch.

"Jo Harrington has been teaching you?" Marie raised a brow as she motioned him to flick the butt into the garden—something his mother would never approve of.

"Miss Jo's been tutoring me this summer." Knowing he couldn't say more, Ernest left it at that.

"I don't recall Jo being studious, but she was gifted in other ways. What does she see in you that you don't share with others?"

He rubbed his sweaty palms on the knees of his pants, refusing to meet Marie's gaze.

"There's an extraordinariness about you, Ernie. Your society girl should be honored you desire her."

Ernest looked up imploringly. "Good, because I only want Louisa."

Marie's smile widened. "The youngest Davenport? They're a pretty bunch, but I'm glad it's not one of the older two. Their mother was defective, but Frederick Davenport's second wife has proven to be a survivor. She already has another husband lined up, freshly arrived from Italy mere months after Frederick's passing, though it's rather scandalous."

"Do you know him? Is he a good man?"

"I understand your concern, but most would say Claudio De Fiore *was* a good man, though many more would call him wicked."

Ernest sighed. "I know what it's liked to be gossiped about because of your parents."

"The ladies around town don't talk about Louisa because of her parents."

"But they talk of her?"

"I won't hide it from you, Ernie. There have been some snide things said about her this past year. The older two Davenport girls matured early. The eldest is an embarrassment to her family and the whole city, moving in with that artist last year in Fairhope like she did. She has hopped from man to man on the Eastern Shore like she's nothing more than a domestic prostitute. Bethany is turning out decently, but she was always a meek girl. All eyes are on which way the youngest will turn."

"Why?" Ernest asked.

"She's forever running about with the Melling sons and Horatio Adams. After the antics of her oldest half-sister, people are expecting the worst."

"But they're like brothers or cousins."

"Then why did Simon react in jealousy against you at Van Antwerp's Saturday night?"

Ernest's eyes widened.

Marie laughed. "Yes, I heard all about that. Dr. Woodslow is my other brother-in-law, and my oldest sister, Grace Anne, helped comfort Louisa when they escorted the group to the hospital."

"She defended me in front of them at the soda fountain."

"But not at the hospital. I suggest you wait until she's not around the boys to speak to her again."

"She'll be at Mobile High School with me next month. Only Horatio will be there out of the three."

"Then plan for that. As for your tutoring, if you really wish it, an encore showing of 'The Shiek' with Rudolph Valentino is Wednesday at The Crown. It's several years old. Have you seen it?"

"My mom wouldn't let me the last time it played."

"You're plenty old enough now, Ernie. Meet me there for the last show of the night and then we can discuss the animal magnetism that actor has on screen."

"I'm restricted this week. I had to get special permission to go across the street to listen to a radio program with my friend."

"So this is what listening to a radio program at your friend's house looks like?" she teased.

Ernest grinned and shrugged.

"You're a clever young man. I'm sure you can find a way to meet me there. I'll sit in the back, and we can talk things over afterward."

"That sounds good. Thank you, Marie."

"I'm looking forward to helping you, Ernie."

Knowing it was too late to go by the Mellings' house, Ernest turned toward home. He slipped inside the front and quietly latched the door behind him. Only the dim light in the hall was on. Clicking it off signaled Sunny to join him from the dark parlor. His cat padded down the bare wood floor, pausing in the hall outside his parents' bedroom.

"Jim!" His mother's soft voice carried through the night, followed by the low rumble of Jim's laughter.

Ernest hurried to shower, then pulled on clean underdrawers and laid on his bed. The ceiling fan spinning above him created a hypnotizing rhythm that flashed images through his mind of Louisa crying over Simon.

***

Wednesday morning, Ernest held a basket with a couple honeybuns and a dozen cinnamon cookies in his lap as his dad drove to Miss Eilands' house.

When the Ford pulled to a stop in front of the gate, his father turned to him. "Tell Miss Eilands hello from me. I'll see y'all this evening."

"Yes, sir."

Miss Eilands was waiting in the kitchen with a pot of coffee.

"There you are, little mister." She motioned to the cup at the empty chair, a cat sitting beside it on the table. "Pour yourself some and share with me whatever it is that smells so good."

"Honeybuns and cookies. My mom woke early to bake before the heat struck too heavy." Ernest collected two plates from the cabinet and served Miss Eilands one of each item. "Jim says hello."

Once he settled across from her, Ernest popped a cookie into his mouth. Miss Eilands tilted her head as though studying him, but her pupils were barely visible through the haze on her eyes.

"I got to thinking last night, little mister."

"Yes, ma'am?"

"Those articles in the newspaper you read out loud to me yesterday—the ones about the vigilante trials—I think that's why Jim sent you to me."

"I guess you're comparing me to that orphaned teenager they flogged. Jim is always talking about safeguarding my abilities." He took another cookie.

"Jimmy is intelligent, even if his feelings often get in the way of his better judgement."

Ernest couldn't help smiling at hearing someone call out his dad's weakness when he was typically praised to a point Ernest knew he'd never measure up to the perceived perfection.

"Those men up north beat that boy within an inch of his life, little mister. Let's hope justice is properly served."

"Jim is always harping about justice." Ernest said with a pinch of spite. "But unfair things happen all the time."

"That's part of why he became a police officer. Jimmy wants to keep people safe—especially his family and friends." She dunked a cookie into her coffee to soften it, then slowly chewed before speaking again. "Life is a series of battles, little mister. Don't get hurt over something within your control."

"Yes, ma'am," he said, unsure of how else to respond to her remark.

"And whatever it is you're doing tonight, it will be successful."

Ernest's mouth went slack before he remembered to keep chewing. He'd been nervous about getting out of the house, but now knew he'd make it to the theater to meet Marie, no matter what.

All morning, he scrubbed the neglected back bedroom that had been inhabited by cats the past several years—maybe even decades. The smell was terrible, but it didn't phase Ernest. He thought of sitting in the theater, learning how to attract

Louisa through the example of Rudolph Valentino. His lunch was half-tasted and barely endured. He resumed cleaning without a glance at the clock. Knowing work would pass the time quicker was all the fuel he needed.

Ernest was scrubbing the farthest corner when he heard heavy footsteps enter the room. He staggered upright, not having realized his body was stiff from prolonged kneeling.

"You look worn out, son. I doubt the floor has been uncovered since before you were born."

"Yeah, it was tough."

"Ready to go home?"

"Yes, sir. I'll be showering and going to bed."

"That sounds like a good plan for everyone. It's too hot for anything else."

At home, Ernest washed thoroughly before coming to the supper table. Baxter had spent the day with the Paterson kids and chattered about all they did in the yard involving pans of water and newspaper boats.

"And Nathan doesn't mind them turning newspapers into playthings?" their dad asked.

Their mother laughed. "So long as one of his editorials aren't on it, but those are only in the Sunday papers now that he has his radio program."

Thinking about what Marie had mentioned the other night, Ernest caught Jim's eye. "Are the teen gangs as bad as people say?"

He finished chewing a piece of fish. "Yes, unfortunately. The kids in the poor neighborhoods are antsy in the heat, beating those they think are beneath them when they can get away with it. I was a nuisance in my neighborhood as a kid, but nothing like this." He looked at his sons. "I never want to hear anything like that about either of you. It's not worth it and it's not even fun."

"Then why did you do it, Daddy?" Baxter asked.

"Because I thought looking tough would get people to respect me." Their father's gaze switched from Baxter to Ernest before he continued. "It didn't. The only path to respect is through exemplifying characteristics like integrity and compassion."

Baxter shrugged. "I don't know what those big words mean."

"They're what your father is," their mother answered with a smile. "Just look to him as an example."

Their parents exchanged loving glances, then she focused on Ernest.

"Jim said the house is looking great, and Miss Eilands is pleased with the extra company."

"I'm tuckered out today."

"I bet, working like that in this heat. Don't worry about helping with the dishes tonight. If you see that Baxter gets a bath, Jim can help me in the kitchen."

Ten minutes later, Ernest shut off the tap in the bathtub as his brother climbed into the water. He planned to help with the dishes so he could get his parents into their room quicker, but stopped in the kitchen doorway. Jim stood behind Francesca at the sink, arms around her. Ernest felt Jim's radiant love fill the space with a cozy warmth that made the summer temperatures pale but somehow cooled the soul. He had noticed that sensation daily since Jim had pointed out his ability. Looking back, Ernest knew that love and protection had been with him since he stayed with Miss Fran after his parents' deaths because Jim had watched over him from that first night.

Once Jim was reading to Baxter and their mother was in the shower, Ernest laid on his bed to wait for the house to quiet. Sunny stretched out by his feet, a rumbling purr broadcasting contentment. To pass the time, Ernest floated a model airplane around his room. Concentrating on the aerial acrobatics kept him from over-thinking what was to come.

An hour later, Ernest opened his door while still on the bed so he could listen if anyone was about. Nothing. Just to be sure, he flew the airplane down the hall and back. With no response to the flying object, Ernest landed it on his desk and grabbed his shoes. He didn't stop to put them on until he was on the back stoop. Then he dashed for Government Street.

He ran all the way to the cathedral. Pausing by the iron fence, he righted his clothing and hair before walking the final block down Dauphin Street.

Ernest handed all his money to the ticket booth operator, then slipped into the darkened theater. The feature had already begun. Ernest waited for his eyes to adjust to the gloom and carefully made his way to Marie while the bellowing organ overpowered the clicking of the film projector. Smiling beneath the brim of her low-fitting hat, Marie patted his knee when he claimed the seat beside her.

He sat in rapture the next hour. The words on the screen matched the tone set by the actors, but their body language surpassed everything—including the dramatic music.

Ernest was disappointed when Marie signaled for him to leave. He wanted to experience everything in the final scene. Instead, he heard the clapping as they walked out the front door. The traffic on Dauphin Street was winding down, but Marie led them south a block. Once they were walking west on Conti, she spoke.

"What did you think, Ernie?"

"It was terrific. I'm sorry I missed the opening."

"You got all the exciting parts. Is it all right if we walk back rather than take the streetcar?"

"Sure," Ernest said, relieved as he hadn't thought to grab a token.

She offered a cigarette and they both lit up.

After a few drags, she spoke. "What do you think is Rudolph Valentino's magnetism to women?"

"His eyes."

"Valentino and Gary Cooper are great examples of men who know what a single look can do."

"I've seen a couple of Cooper's westerns."

"Good." Marie turned so she was walking backward. "Let me see you look at me. Not just look, but gaze with longing."

Ernest stopped on the sidewalk and stared at Marie.

"With feeling, Ernie. You've got dark lashes around your blue eyes, like Gary Cooper. Put them to work." Marie tucked her cigarette between her lips. "Drop your chin a little so you can look up from under your brow. Now part your mouth a little and let the hint of a smile play at the corner of your lips."

If those guys who jumped him in the cemetery or those girls who dismissed him on the streetcar when Ernest went downtown with Theodore could see him out with a society woman, maybe they'd stop thinking of him as the murder kid.

"You did well, but keep practicing." Marie started walking again.

"But won't it come naturally if I'm looking at a girl I really desire?"

"I should be offended, Ernie."

"I didn't mean it like that. You're truly pretty Miss Marley, but my brain is full of Louisa."

She laughed. "Jim used to fill my head the way Louisa is filling yours. I was a couple years older than you, and he was everything my young heart wanted. When he got me the chance to play the organ at the Lyric for a matinee film, I thought there would never be another man for me as long as I lived."

"What happened between you two?"

"When I made my debut, my social schedule filled with masquerades, parties, and charity events that Winnie and Jim would never be invited to. But Jim was busy learning the ways of the police department. He made it to a couple of my piano recitals, and I to a few suppers at the apartment house, but I didn't sit around pining."

As they approached Broad Street, Ernest noticed the silhouette of a policeman standing watch at the corner.

"Dammit," he muttered. Ernest dropped the cigarette, stepped on it, and nodded up the block.

"Do you know him?" Marie asked.

"I'm not sure yet, but even if I don't know him by name, all the officers know me. We can't turn around because then he'll think something is wrong."

Marie stared at Ernest a moment before plunking her hat on his head and tugging it around his ears. Then she grabbed him by the wrist and marched toward the policeman.

"Why you little…." She grumbled as they approached. "Wait until your mother sees what you've done. My sister will give you a tongue lashing like you've never had before!"

Ernest kept his head down, but saw the officer's black shoes turn towards them.

"Excuse us, officer," Marie said with irritability in her voice. "I need to get my nephew home. The things boys get into these days!"

She was headed south on Broad Street when he called out, "Anything I can be of assistance with, Miss?"

Ernest's heart leapt into his throat as she stopped and turned back. "I don't believe so, officer, unless you want the chance to laugh over the bald spot he's got on his head. At least he'll never play with a lighter again."

Marie reached for her hat on Ernest's head.

"Please, no, auntie! I don't need no officer laughing at me!" Ernest wriggled on the end of Marie's grip as he held the hat to his head.

"Go, on home, folks," the officer said with a chuckle.

Marie set a quick pace, keeping hold of Ernest's wrist until they were across Government Street.

"You were perfect." She released him and slowed. "And if the officer happened to recognize me, he'll know I have a couple nephews."

They walked the next few blocks in silence, skirting the edge of the neighborhood along Government. At the corner of George Street, Marie stopped in the shadows of the oak trees.

Ernest handed her the hat. "Thank you for helping me understand how magnetism works."

"I'll be home all weekend. Stop in if you have questions. Let me get my key while you're with me so I don't have to search my purse while I'm alone." She opened her handbag and rummaged through the contents before pulling out a rusty key.

"That looks old," Ernest remarked.

"It's original to the house and very fragile."

After she said the words, the key slipped from her hand. Ernest was a step too far away, but he reached out with his hand and mind, causing the key to float toward him rather than fall.

He curled his fingers around it as horror struck. Marie would see him as a monster. A bead of sweat ran down the side of his face as he stood frozen in the sticky air.

"Ernie." Her voice was as soft as the touch of her fingers on his fisted hand. She waited until he met her eyes. "Thank you for saving it."

His brows drew together, holding her kind gaze. "You— you're welcome."

Ernest opened his hand palm up, fingers relaxing like talons on an osprey.

"I always knew you were extraordinary," she said with a smile. "Goodnight."

Eleven

Jim looked forward to having Sunday and Monday off after the long, hot week and his current Saturday night patrol. What was it about summer that made everyone drive like jackasses? He had pulled over no less than thirty vehicles for varying infractions from not having their lights on to failing to stop at a stop sign, all before nine that night. With three hours to go on his shift, the roads were finally clearing. Jim used a callbox to check-in at the station before cruising through Washington Square. He wanted to make sure all was well in the neighborhood before it got to an hour that his motorcycle would be bothersome to people trying to sleep.

He turned off the main road onto Rapier, passing the Farleys' house and coasting onto Palmetto. Glancing to his right at the next intersection, he nearly tipped the Harley-Davidson when he saw Ernest smoking and laughing on the front porch of the Marleys' house.

After hastily parking, Jim strode across the lawn. Ernest jumped to his feet when Jim stopped at the foot of the front steps, the cigarette mysteriously gone. Jim saw the panic in his face beneath the nonchalant façade he was trying to pull off.

"You need to get home, Ernest."

"Mom said I could stay out until ten."

"Now, son." He didn't raise his voice, but seeing the look of fear flash through Ernest's eyes was enough to know his low, calm voice was more terrifying than raging shouts.

"Goodnight, Miss Marie," Ernest said before hastily descending the stairs.

"Goodnight, Ernie. Thank you for stopping by." She smiled as she watched him leave. When she looked at Jim, the grin was still plastered on her face.

"Stay away from my son."

"Since when is it an issue for neighbors to stop and chat? People do that daily."

"Then why did he look guilty?"

"Just what are you implying, Officer Abbott?" She stood and looked down at him with disdain from the porch. "It's not as if I had him inside the house with me. We were in plain view of a public corner."

He crossed his arms. "I'm not implying anything yet, Marie, but I reckon you're up to something."

"Because a neighbor stopped to say hello?"

"Not just any neighbor," Jim said she he stepped onto the first stair, "but my son. And you've been asking a lot of questions about him lately."

"And your point is?"

"Just that you appeared awfully chummy with him— complete with cigarettes—for a casual stop."

"You must see women as being incapable of having a friendship without sex getting involved. But I guess after you flaunted your intimate relationship with Francesca at Sadie's party, I shouldn't be surprised."

"Francesca is my wife." Jim advanced another step so he was eye-level with Marie. "But if I ever witness or so much as hear about you talking with my son again, you're not going to like the repercussions."

Jim stalked to his motorcycle and drove home to make sure Ernest had followed directions.

Francesca met him in the parlor doorway, hand on his sleeve as she leaned in for a kiss. "I wasn't expecting to see you until after midnight."

"I wanted to make sure Ernest returned."

"He came in a minute ago." She studied Jim's face and raised a finger to the tight line of his mouth, ruffling the edge of his mustache. "What is it, Jim?"

He kissed her fingertip, keeping hold of her hand as he lowered it. "Ernest isn't to leave the house without me for the next two days. I'll figure out what to do with him after that."

"What happened?" Francesca's tone was tight with worry. "And what can I do to help?"

"I can't talk now, but stay awake if you can and listen out for him."

"I will, Jim. Don't let this distract you." A soft hand cupped his cheek. "Take a moment to calm down, to feel."

Nodding, he closed his eyes and held her hands in each of his. Jim felt her concern and knew Francesca worried most when he worked nights. Focusing on her love, he worked to fill her soul with warmth of his own so it overshadowed the fear with hope.

When he opened his eyes, Francesca's were shimmering with emotion. He planted a kiss on her lips and whispered, "I'll make it home later, Francesca, I promise."

When he paused at the stop sign at Government, an open-topped fiver full of laughing young men flew by, heading towards town. Jim huffed, flicked on the toggle for his siren, and sped after them. Government Street was a blur as the raggedy car picked up speed, slowing only to turn left onto Washington Avenue, then cut a tight right turn onto Dauphin Street. Amid the heavy flow of pedestrians in the entertainment district, people jumped aside, many narrowly escaping being hit by the automobile.

Another wailing motorcycle fell in behind Jim. Now that Officer Murphy was involved, Jim pushed ahead, coming up on the left side of the vehicle to wave them over. He received three middle fingers and a tossed bottle that shattered on the road beside him.

Jim's position forced the driver to turn right when they got to the end of Dauphin. Hooking south on Water Street, running parallel to the Mobile River, he sped beside the car.

Their last-second right turn onto Government Street caused Jim to veer onto the sidewalk before deftly maneuvering back onto the road. Crossing behind the car, Jim raced to block the right side of the automobile, keeping them from going back into the busy area.

In response, the driver yanked the steering wheel left as though to flip a U-turn, losing control as they crossed the streetcar tracks. The jalopy swerved before jumping the concrete curb and striking the stairs to the courthouse building with a crunch. Steam released from under the crumpled hood.

A passenger in brown pants and a beige shirt jumped out of the backseat. Jim cut his engine and climbed off his motorcycle. In his haste, the bike fell over before he could set the kickstand. With a quick glance to make sure Officer Murphy was there to deal with the guys still in the car, Jim ran down the side of the courthouse after the escapee. The young man turned west on Church Street and increased his lead.

"Stop, police!" Jim shouted as he put in a burst of heightened effort.

His hat fell off as he passed Christ Church, but Jim puffed and pushed harder as sweat rolled down his face.

The fleeing man made to turn into the residential area to the south, which led to a plethora of alleys and other hiding spots. Jim surged forward with a tackle Alvin Farley might have appreciated. The young man yelped when Jim landed on him.

"Get off me!"

"You're under arrest." Jim panted as he wrangled his handcuffs out. He clicked them into place around the guy's wrists and stood.

"I think you broke my ribs." The young man's breath expelled the fiery scent of shinny.

"Does it feel tender," Jim asked in fake concern, "a dull ache where you landed?"

"Yeah, sure does."

"It's called mild bruising. You'll be fine." Jim walked half a step behind him, gripping his upper right arm and nudging him up Joachim Street towards Government so they could return to the crash site. After his breathing slowed, he spoke again. "What were y'all up to tonight?"

"Just a bit of fun."

An automobile pulled alongside them, the passengers hooting and pointing as the driver honked.

Jim waved his free hand to shoo them away as they continued their walk. "I'm Officer Abbott. What's your name?"

"Dave."

"Did you have fun, Dave?"

"I did until you landed on top of me."

"You shouldn't have fled the scene of the accident. That's one charge against you right there, not to mention evading arrest. How old are you and your friends?"

"Eighteen, or thereabouts."

"Whose car is it, Dave?"

"Some fella on Houston Street, as far as I know. We borrowed it to get downtown."

"You got downtown all right, and you'll be staying in jail for using a car without consent, among your other infractions. Which one of you threw that bottle at me?"

Dave laughed. "I only gave you the finger."

"We'll find out who it was soon enough."

The courthouse was a block beyond the police station on the opposite side of Government Street. Word—or the sound of the crash itself—must have traveled straight to headquarters because the shift lieutenant and a sergeant were standing in front of the stone steps where the three other boys from the wrecked car sat like toads on a log, their hands cuffed.

"Add him to the others, Abbott," the lieutenant told Jim, "then step over here with me."

Jim did as he was commanded.

"I heard Murphy's account before he left to inform the jail of their increasing numbers, but give me your side from when you first spotted the vehicle."

Recounting the chase from the time he left George Street, Jim included the route they drove, Officer Murphy joining the chase, the thrown bottle, and his maneuvers to keep the car from going back toward the crowds.

"And what of your bike?" The lieutenant motioned to the Harley-Davidson, now propped respectfully beside Officer Murphy's. "Word is you fell when you ran after the boy."

"The bike tipped when I dismounted, but I didn't fall. I was in a hurry to catch the kid, so I didn't pick it up."

"You're all right?"

"Yes, sir. A bit winded is all. I haven't had to run like that for a while—especially in riding boots." Jim wiped his sleeve over his damp forehead.

"Where's your hat?"

"It fell off on Church Street."

"Go get it—on foot—while we wait for the wagon."

"Yes, Lieutenant."

Jim walked along the side of the courthouse, taking his time so he could cool off a little. Gazing up as he passed under Judge Spunner's chamber window, he thought of Jo's words about how the judge had unknowingly poisoned his police career. Jim hoped she never expressed that to the judge because Jim was grateful for all he had done for him in other respects.

Jim's hat should have been just beyond the St. Emanuel Street intersection, but the street was empty. His eyes skimmed the shadowed ground next to Christ Church as he advanced.

"Looking for this, Officer Abbott?" The hardened delinquent from the other day leaned against the iron fence on the far side of an oak tree, Jim's uniform hat sitting cockeyed on his dark curls.

"As a matter of fact I am, Ryan."

He frowned, most likely annoyed Jim had remembered who he was.

Jim came within a couple feet and extended his hand. "I appreciate you collecting it for me."

"Who says I'm going to give it back? Ninety-six might be my lucky number." Ryan removed the hat and fingered the eagle medallion on the crown.

Jim wondered what Ryan's aura looked like. The idea of having Deborah's mediumship abilities as a way of shifting out guilty people while on patrol was tempting, but then he remembered the disorientating sensation Jo's astral projection placed on him the few times he had experienced it. He was content to stay as he was. Expanding his aura was helpful without the bombardment of everyone's colors or the stomach-churning sensation of floating away from himself.

"If you refuse to return it, you could be charged with theft of property." Jim lowered his hand and settled back half a step. "I'll warn you there's a lieutenant on the next block who dislikes dealing with juveniles and sticks them with the toughest charge to keep them away longer."

"I ain't a kid." Ryan surged forward, shoving the hat against Jim's chest. "I'm eighteen as of last month, but you won't see me around these parts much longer."

"What are your plans, Ryan?"

"Something better than working on the docks, in a sweaty warehouse, or playing Little Boy Blue on a motorcycle," he smirked before striding west.

Jim brushed off his hat and turned back to the courthouse as he donned it.

***

Jim arrived home at half-past midnight, locked the door behind him, and hung his hat. Flicking off the hallway light, he advanced toward the soft glow of the kitchen as he worked open his jacket buttons. Francesca sat at the little table in a pale cotton nightgown, a cup of tea and a book before her. Her smile when she stood bestowed healing balm to his soul. Arms around her waist, Jim hugged her without speaking.

After several minutes, he pulled away. "I'm sorry, baby. I must be as damp and smelly as I am tired. Lord knows I only like late nights when I'm dancing or making love with you."

"I'm ready if you are." She began swaying, eyes bright with hope.

"I can't right now. If I didn't need a shower, I'd fall into bed."

"Shower and then draw a bath to soak in for a bit. I'll listen for the water to shut off and bring you a bite to eat."

"Thanks, Fran."

A quarter of an hour later, he was in the clawfoot tub, a rolled towel on the back ledge to rest his head on while he let the warm water relax his body. The bathroom door opened and Francesca slipped in. She balanced a tray on the sink and turned to Jim with a glass tumbler holding a couple inches of amber liquid.

He sat up, water sloshing the sides of the tub. "Is that Irish whiskey?"

She smiled as she handed it to him.

"How did—"

"Drink first, Jim."

He wanted to take it slow, but after the comforting burn of the first half, he slung back the rest and settled against his makeshift pillow with contentment. "God bless you, Francesca."

"Do you want your sandwich now?" She asked as she set the empty glass on the tray.

"I want to enjoy this feeling for a while. I haven't had whiskey in my belly in far too long."

Francesca placed a folded towel on the tile floor and sat alongside the bathtub, facing Jim. Her closest arm propped on the side before she reached the hand to his. Grinning, he brought her fingers to his lips for a kiss, then lowered their linked hands to the water as he gazed at her.

"How did you acquire it?"

"I called in an order."

Jim's eyes widened with surprise. "Don't tell me you've done this enough times to have a supplier."

"No, but several years back, Sean discreetly told me if you ever had a rough day that I couldn't help you with to telephone and ask if you could borrow his Louisville Slugger. After you checked on Ernest, I called. Sean laughed and said it was about time. He showed up a quarter of an hour later with a serving."

"Then God bless Judge Spunner, too." Jim gave a satisfied sigh. "I was just thinking a few hours back that I owe much to him. Did Ernest give you any trouble after he got home?"

"No, and he's still in bed. I checked both boys not long before you got here. What happened with Ernest?" Francesca's countenance was a mixture of love and concern.

"I drove the neighborhood to check things before it got too late. He was sitting on the Marleys' front porch."

Her eyebrows narrowed. "Alone?"

"With Marie. They were smoking and laughing like old friends."

"Marie? Sadie told me she was going across the bay with her family and their mother this week."

"Well, she's home."

"She's a dozen years older than Ernest. What on earth can she want with him?"

"I think she might know."

"Know?" When the realization struck, fear paled her face. "But how? Sean swore Dr. Woodslow wouldn't talk."

"With Marie living in the neighborhood and Ernest not being discreet, people are bound to see something unordinary and pass it along on a porch visit. You know how rumors run around Washington Square. Marie is intelligent, even if she plays flippant. I think she was after information about Ernest the times she's spoken with me recently, and that was before the Van Antwerp situation. People must have been talking about Ernest all summer." He wanted to add that everything was Jo's fault, but held his tongue. "I'll be home the next two days. After that, it's extra hours with the Buyers' Week events, but we'll figure out something."

Jim rubbed the washcloth over his face as though he could clear his head with the motion. When he opened his eyes, Francesca dabbed the moisture from his face with a towel, gently rubbing at his mustache before leaning over the side of the tub to kiss him. He grinned, eyes trailing from his wife's face to the V-cut of her neckline.

Francesca stood and stepped into the bath without hesitation. Not bothering to disrobe, she settled on his lap and curled against his chest as though they were cuddling on the sofa. The water from him had wetted the top of her nightgown, causing the blush-colored cotton to cling to her skin.

Jim kissed her forehead. "Nearly seven years and you still surprise me."

"I'm as in love with you as I was when we first met, Jim."

"Not me, Francesca. I love you at least ten times more."

Jim took her mouth in a deep kiss while an exploratory touch roamed her nightgown. What wasn't wet before was dripping by the time his hand worked between her thighs. Seeing Francesca's pleasure bloom made enduring the trials of the night worth every discomfort. She deserved all the pleasure he could give her—now and always. After she crested with beauty only he was fortunate enough to witness, he held her as her heartbeat slowed.

"It's your turn, Jim." She trailed a hand across his stomach.

"I'm exhausted, baby."

"What happened at work?"

Francesca relaxed against him and as he told about the dozens of drivers needing citations, the automobile chase that ended in a foot pursuit, and the final hour that included a brawl outside a speakeasy on Dauphin Street he happened to pass when attempting to get coffee with Officer Murphy.

"I'm glad you had Happy with you those final hours."

"The worst day at work is more bearable with someone to laugh about it with." Jim kissed her neck. "And even better with a devoted wife to return to."

"I love you, Jim. Thank you for keeping your promise to make it home."

"Always, babydoll."

Twelve

The next morning, Jim woke to the aroma of coffee, sausage, and biscuits just after seven-thirty. Fearing something was wrong—Francesca typically did a simple breakfast on Sundays—Jim hurried to the kitchen.

His wife greeted him with a smile. "Good morning."

"Morning." Jim looked at Baxter enjoying the food at the table and smiled at his son before approaching Francesca. His arms went around the apron that protected her sky-blue church dress as he kissed her cheek. "Is everything okay?"

"I thought you'd be hungry after your late night, especially since you're driving us downtown for Mass."

"I am?" With his schedule being like it was, Jim only made it to Mass once a month—less if he took his Sundays off for fishing instead of attending. "But I was going to—"

"If people are talking about Ernest," she said while holding eye contact, "the best thing we can do is show that we're still the same church-going people we've always been."

Jim understood her point and nodded, though he thought giving Ernest the chance to see Marie wasn't ideal.

Francesca woke their eldest while Jim got shaved and suited.

After breakfast, Ernest and Baxter sat in the bed of the pickup truck on the way to Mass. Jim parked a couple blocks from the cathedral, placed his fedora on his head, and let the boys walk ahead of them as he held Francesca's hand.

"They've both grown a lot this summer," she remarked. "Ernest looks more like a man every day."

"I know it and have told him as much recently."

"We have two intelligent, handsome, and caring sons. Thank you for encouraging and guiding them."

"I know your love and nurturing does more for them than I ever could." Jim led Francesca through the back gate of the cathedral property.

Under the shade of the portico, Francesca fell into conversation with Mrs. Wolf and her son—Jo's stepmother and half-brother. Jim's gaze roamed the crowd for potential dangers. If gossips were the worst thing out there, a flock surrounded them from Mrs. Wolf on the south to Dr. Woodslow on the north and every decked-out busybody in between. Several people appeared to be watching Ernest, who was down by the front gate with Baxter, and one mother even pulled her child away when he tried to talk to Baxter.

Judge Spunner approached Jim with a grin as bright as his pastel seersucker suit.

"Good morning, Jim." The judge pumped his hand. "It's always great to see you at Mass. Francesca is much too pretty to be around town alone so often, even if the whole police force keeps an eye on her."

Francesca linked her arm around Jim's as she joined them. "I can hold my own, thank you very much. Jim, did you tell Sean what's going on?"

Jim shook his head.

"Francesca, darling, allow me to stroll the grounds with you before Mass begins." Judge Spunner offered his arm accompanied by a flamboyant bow and escorted her down the steps through the crowd that parted for him.

"Daddy!" Baxter threw his arms around Jim's middle as Ernest stopped beside them. "There's going to be a picnic next Saturday on the bay. Can we go?"

"I'm working Saturday, so we'll have to ask your mother if she'll take you."

"I could bring him," Ernest offered.

"We'll see, son." Jim said, unsure how the week would playout. He took Baxter's hand and clapped Ernest's shoulder as he moved to the door. "Let's get our seats. "

Once Jim and the boys were in their customary pew in the back third of the cathedral, Judge Spunner and Francesca joined them.

He greeted Baxter on Jim's far side, then Ernest. "Are you ready for another year of school, Ernest?" he asked as Francesca sat between Ernest and Jim.

"Yes, Judge Spunner. The new high school campus is terrific, even if it takes longer to get there."

"If you ever need a refreshment on your way to the streetcar in the afternoons, stop in my house. Hattie would be pleased to host you and any of your friends, but if she's not there, Althea would see to things."

"Thank you, sir," he said before the judge walked away.

Jim took a deep breath, rebalanced his hat on his lap, and settled back against the wooden pew as the organ music started. His right arm was around Baxter's shoulders and he clasped Francesca's hand in his left, causing her to turn to him. The delicate shadows the lace mantilla painted on her cheek were like a work of art. He mouthed the words "I love you." Francesca radiant smile melted the remainder of his stress while the deep chords of the organ rumbled his soul.

Ten minutes into the service, Ernest started hiccuping. He kept a hand over his mouth, but he still shook with each disturbance. After a minute, Francesca whispered for him to step outside.

Jim sat for five seconds as the priest droned on, then practically leapt to his feet, clutching his fedora. He slipped out the door and donned his hat.

Just as he suspected, Ernest stood at the foot of the steps as though waiting for someone, not a hiccup to be heard. Jim stepped behind one of the massive interior columns that were spaced along the center of the portico, matching the exterior ones.

A minute later, the front gate opened.

"I had hoped to find you here when I saw the truck gone," Marie said, "though I wasn't sure if Jim had taken you fishing."

"Miss Fran wanted us to go to Mass. I'm sorry I had to leave early last night." Ernest climbed the steps as they spoke while Jim battled between breaking up the liaison or listening to learn more. "Did you hear about the staffing situation?"

"Yes, and he trusts my judgment. Payment would be in the mid-range of what we spoke of. Think about it, all right?"

Jim shifted around the column as they neared him to stay hidden from their view.

"Yes, ma'am."

"Stop by in a few days, Ernie, and let me know your decision. Now hurry back before one of your parents come looking for you."

As soon as the cathedral door shut behind Ernest, Jim strode toward Marie. "I told you to stay away from my son."

Marie turned from where she was poised to descend the steps, the grip on the handle of her purse straining white around her knuckles. "I was only greeting a neighbor."

"Neighbors don't discuss payments."

"It's no concern of yours, Jim Abbott."

"The hell it isn't!"

She sighed and glanced left, feigning boredom. "Francesca keeps such a pristine yard, when I leaned Ernest helps with the yardwork, I thought about hiring him to work our property."

"You're still a lousy liar, Marie."

With a playful lift of her shoulder, a smirk graced her face. "At least I recognize a good thing when I see it."

Jim stalked down the stairs after her, but knew he couldn't stop her as she exited the gate. He lit a cigarette and paced the walkway at the base of the steps until the first wave of parishioners exited.

On the portico, he went to Francesca's side as soon as she appeared with the boys. To answer Francesca's questioning look, Jim whispered, "He was meeting up with Marie. She knows, baby."

Francesca's face set in determined firmness. "We're going home," she declared and ushered the boys down the side steps, Jim following.

At the house, Francesca kept charge. "Change out of your church clothes and play in your rooms until I holler that lunch is ready."

Jim hung his suit jacket and hat before following Francesca into the kitchen.

"It's not safe for Ernest to be in town," Francesca said as she washed her hands. "Go ask Jo if she'll put me and the boys up until you get through Buyers' Week. That way you can focus on your job without worrying about Ernest."

"Is Jo even home?"

"She typically is on Sundays as it's one of the only days she has uninterrupted time with Cyrus."

Knowing how precious time with a spouse was, Jim was reluctant. "I don't want to bother them."

"Jo will understand the importance."

Jim drove his pickup to Spring Hill and parked in front of the Harringtons' house. The door opened before he could ring the bell.

Jo crossed her arms over the red blouse she wore. "What brings you here, Jim?"

"I've come to request that you guard Francesca and the boys here for the week."

"Guard?" Jo led Jim into the house. "What's going on?"

"Marie Marley is after Ernest. I don't know what her ulterior motives are, but she knows of his abilities and has offered him money."

"I never expected her to be a cradle robber."

"It's strictly about his abilities from what I can tell, but he snuck out of Mass this morning to see her after I broke up their meeting on her porch last night." Jim slumped onto the chaise in the library. "I'll be working nonstop come Tuesday with Buyers' Week details and know I can't watch Ernest properly during all that. Would you host them here and make sure Ernest has no contact with outsiders?"

"You know I will," she said with uncharacteristic softness. "Bring them over tomorrow at noon. Sarah will have a luncheon for all of us."

"Thank you." He gave her a quick hug. "And I'm sorry if I've been a jackass to you lately."

"*If?*" Jo laughed. "I'll see you tomorrow, Jim."

Back at home, Baxter was napping, so Jim called Ernest and Francesca into the parlor. Ernest kept his gaze averted from Francesca when he sat on the opposite side of the sofa.

"We need to know we can trust you, Ernest," Jim said as he claimed the chair across from them. "Your actions this week haven't supported a case for us doing so."

"Sorry," he mumbled. "But I needed to finish the conversation with my friend."

"Why do you think Marie Marley is your friend when she's doing things that have you lying to your parents?"

"I have questions, and she's willing to answer them."

"I'm always willing to help, Ernest," Francesca spoke before Jim could say the same thing.

"No offense, Mom, but not about this."

"Then your father?"

Ernest shook his head, a wave of hair falling over his eyes.

"What are your questions about?" Francesca prodded. "What can't you talk to us about that you can discuss with a practical stranger?"

He shrugged.

"Is this about the Davenport girl?" Jim asked, leaning forward, his elbows resting on his knees. When Ernest nodded, Jim continued. "Your mom knows about girls, and I know what it's like to be your age and have an eye on one."

"But not like Louisa. You weren't around folks like her." Ernest looked at Francesca. "And no offense, Mom, but even if you do like to vacation on the bay, you've never been out of the country, and the only dances you go to are private parties or the annual Police Relief Association Ball, not masquerades and society events like her family."

"I *was* a debutante, Ernest." A soft smile curved the corner of Francesca's lip. "Judge Spunner even waltzed with me at a cotillion back when he was a young solicitor. But after my father died, all the parties had to stop for the season. Then my mother took ill, and I left it all behind to care for her."

"Louisa spent spring in Paris, belongs to a swim club, rides horses, weekends across—"

"None of that makes her better than you, son," Jim declared. "I heard the other day her sister is dating a deckhand. If she likes you, the size of your home isn't going to bother her. Any girl who needs you to pretend to be someone else isn't worth having."

"She likes me already, but I need a boost. Some charm and culture to elevate me in her eyes. Marie understands that, even if y'all don't." Ernest sighed. "Can I go to my room now?"

Jim looked at Francesca, who gave a slight nod.

"All right, son."

When they were alone, Francesca looked pleadingly at Jim. "Are young men always this headstrong?"

Jim laughed. "This isn't the worst of it, baby."

Thirteen

Ernest slept late Monday morning, but determined as he dressed to use his abilities as often as possible to further hone his skills. He needed to be ready for whatever Marie asked of him once he was hired as a security guard at her brother-in-law's property. The "murder kid" name would be left behind once he was out of Washington Square. Plus the money he'd bring in would mean new clothes and hopefully a shiny motorcycle that would surely impress Louisa—not to mention everyone else.

Realizing it was going on nine when he walked into the kitchen, concern struck Ernest when he didn't see Baxter.

"It's late. Where's Bax?" he asked as he lowered to his chair.

"Baxter already had breakfast and is with the Farleys this morning," Miss Fran replied. "We pick him up at half-past eleven."

"Could I go over to Jack's house until then?"

"No." Jim nearly snapped the word.

After breakfast and the kitchen work was done, Ernest lay on his bed with a comic book. Sunny slept at his feet beneath the whirling ceiling fan.

"Time to go, son," Jim called out just before eleven-thirty.

"I really have to walk with you?" Ernest asked as he met his parents in the hall.

"We're driving over."

At the Farleys' house, Jim waited behind the wheel as Ernest's mom collected Baxter. The women hugged, then Miss Deborah waved from the porch as Baxter ran ahead. He climbed up and plopped next to Ernest.

"Are we going on vacation?" Baxter asked, looking at the suitcases they were sitting on.

Ernest shrugged.

Rather than heading for home, Jim drove west on Government Street. When he realized they were headed to the Harringtons, Ernest relaxed.

"Looks like you'll get to play with Arabella today," he told Baxter as they braced their feet to keep from sliding as Jim drove up the slope of Old Shell Road.

Baxter grinned.

At the brick mansion, Miss Jo stood on the front steps with her hands on the hips of her white trousers, arms bare in the sun because of her sleeveless blouse. She was barefoot, as usual, but that didn't stop her from walking across the hot driveway. Miss Fran had once remarked that Jo was tough enough to walk on glass since she was a girl, and Ernest believed it.

She stopped at the back of the truck. "Hey there, boys."

"Hi, Miss Jo!" Baxter jumped at her. "Am I here to play with Arabella?"

"Among other things." She lifted him down as easily as Jim could have. "She's waiting for you by the pond."

"Did you get the koi?"

Jo shrugged, her freckled shoulders nearly bronze from her time outdoors. "Why don't you go find out?"

Baxter ran for the house as Ernest climbed out.

"I'm glad y'all are here," she remarked.

"It was a surprise to us, Miss Jo," Ernest replied.

"Clive is waiting for you in the greenhouse."

When Ernest reached the front door, he looked back. Jo was embracing his mother, and Jim was lifting the suitcases out of the back.

"What's going on?" Ernest asked Jim as he carried the luggage into the house. "Are we staying the night so you and Mom can go off?"

"No," Jim said as he set the cases at the foot of the grand stairs. "You boys and your mom are staying the week."

"But I—"

"I've got a vague understanding of what you wanted to do this week, and it's not going to happen. You're here with your mother, Baxter, and some of y'all's closest friends. There's plenty of land to explore, games to play, and experiments to participate in. Enjoy your time in the safety of Spring Hill."

"But Marie isn't dangerous." Ernest threw his hands up in exasperation. "She's helping me!"

"I never claimed to be perfect, son, but I know villainy when I see it."

"Of course you do, Officer Abbott. It's your job, after all."

"I have no desire for a scheming society bitch."

"You're upset about Marie," Ernest chided, "because you liked her when you lived on Hallett Street."

Miss Jo and his mother entered the house with his words, both pausing to watch the exchange.

"I don't know what stories she's filled your head with, son, but I'll tell you three things. One, I was always a gentleman with her when we were around each other except for one time when we both had nipped on some shinny. Two," he said as the accompanying finger raised, "I haven't had a yearning thought about her in over seven years. And three, thanks to her recent actions, I have nothing but loathing for her now. Is that clear?"

"Yes, sir."

"Good," Jo said as she stood directly in front of Ernest. She didn't point or push, though the hardness in her eyes showed she was capable of either of those things—or worse. "I hope that's the only time in your life I hear that tone come out of your mouth directed at one of your parents. I'll not stand for contempt in my house."

"Then I should go because all I have toward Jim is a bad attitude."

Jo stepped closer, the intensity in her soul poised like a lioness. "Anyone would be blessed to have a father that's half as hardworking and involved as Jim is. If Cyrus and I both died tomorrow, I'd want my children to be raised by your parents, not my brother and Del."

Ernest flinched.

"Just give it time, Ernest." Jo's tone matched the softening in her hazel eyes. "Don't try to grow up too quickly."

Ernest shook his head and exited the back door.

In the greenhouse, Clive looked over from the potting bench. "Hey, Ernie. I'm glad you made it. Come see this root system. I've been experimenting with watering patterns to discover which helps ferns thrive the most. This one went crazy."

After several minutes of listening to Clive yap about his watering patterns for each of the shelves, Ernest was put in charge of the row of ferns that were misted only. Squeals and shouts of delight from Arabella and Baxter carried through windows that were cranked open to allow the summer air to circulate through the greenhouse.

"The koi were delivered yesterday. Sage has been teasing Arabella that the foxes who cut through the yard each night will catch them," Clive remarked about his younger sisters. "Dad had to carry Arabella inside last night because she didn't want to leave them."

"Do you think they'll kill the fish?"

"Possibly. They're clever, you know, and the koi are only about six inches long right now. But poor Bella if they do. She'll cry for days."

Ernest knew that if it happened while they were there, Baxter would be just as heartbroken as his friend. He paused misting to watch out an open window when his parents appeared on the veranda. His mother's arms went around Jim's middle, hands resting in the back pockets of his denim trousers.

"My parents are just as bad with their displays," Clive remarked as he wiped his hands on a towel and leaned against the worktable with the ease of his cultured father.

Ernest's face heated, but he knew he might as well question him. "Do you have any experience with girls?"

"More than Brandon Spunner does."

Ernest looked up at his friend at the mention of the younger boy. "I should hope so!"

Clive crossed his arms. "When you're at an all-boys' school like we are, you make up for lost time whenever you're around girls."

"But *Brandon?*" Ernest pictured the judge's oldest son. The few times he'd been at the judge's house, Brandon was at the piano. He was a prodigy of sorts—obsessed with music like Clive was with plants.

"He was getting handsy with a girl at an end-of-the-school-year picnic at the Gulf Fishing and Hunting Club property. He's all about bubs. Me, I check out the girl's legs. The worst thing is a pretty girl with thick ankles."

"Do you know Louisa Davenport?"

Clive whistled. "She's got some good legs thanks to her tall parents. Have you kissed her?"

"What? No!" Ernest's throat went dry. "I mean, I'd like to, but things haven't gotten that far."

"And they aren't likely to, from what I hear." Clive smirked. "The Melling stepbrothers go to a different school than me, but we often ride together at the stables. Simon's set his cap on Louisa and has promised to flatten anyone who makes a move on her. I'd like to see him try that on you."

"He has." Ernest told him about the trip to Van Antwerp's.

"I would have loved to have seen that island rat get what he deserves! He struts around like he's the prince of the Melling family when he's just a stepson. It's Asher that has the right to be cocky, just as Brandon does."

Ernest frowned, thinking he had no claim whatsoever on anything from Jim or Fran. "But how does Spunner get girls to let him touch them?"

"He serenades them with songs he makes up on the spot. His perfect pitch and dimpled grin woo them, along with the fact that he learned the art of flirtation at an early age from watching his father. According to my mom, the old judge is shameless."

"And Brandon just touched that girl in the middle of a co-ed picnic?"

Clive laughed. "You public school kids have a lot to learn. There's always a spot you can get to. That time, the petting area was a thicket of trees along Dog River. The girls' school chaperones were told a snake was seen in that area, so they kept away."

"What were you doing there?"

"What do you think, Ernie?"

Annoyed Clive didn't give details, Ernest crossed his arms. Clive might not think he was worthy of telling since he wasn't part of the private school scene, but Ernest wasn't going to give him the satisfaction of knowing how much that stung.

***

Dinner with the Harringtons was an emotional affair. Arabella refused to eat. She spent the first five minutes of the meal staring at the sea bass fillet on her plate with tears streaming down her face. Beside her, Baxter held her hand and picked at his own food.

"Try to eat, Arabella," her father coaxed. "Just the vegetables at least."

She wiped her nose with her napkin and shook her head.

"No one will starve from missing one meal," Miss Jo said in between bites.

Baxter patted his friend's arm. "My daddy knows all about fish. He'd know how to protect the koi. Why couldn't he stay, Mommy?"

"He's working long hours the rest of the week. He needs extra rest while he can get it."

"Ernie and I will guard the pond tonight, Bella," Clive told his youngest sister.

"You'll keep the koi safe?"

"Of course," Clive assured her.

"That's impossible." Sage's voice was disparaging. "You can't stop nature."

"I'll protect them," Ernest declared.

"With your magic?" Arabella's hazel eyes brightened.

"Yes, please, Ernie!" Baxter added.

His mother and Jo exchanged glances, but kept quiet as Ernest nodded.

Clive laughed and nudged Ernest's side with his elbow. "This is going to be fun!"

After the dishes were cleared, Clive collected a flashlight and blanket, then led Ernest down the garden path to the pond. The moon was several days away from being full, but the ambient glow allowed them to set up their seating area without using the flashlight.

Ernest sat cross-legged on the blanket as Clive leaned over the pond to check the fish, their bright orange and white bodies shining in the moonlight.

"All seven are accounted for." Clive sat beside Ernest, his voice low. "Now to keep it that way."

"I'll handle it." Ernest went on to tell him how he helped Baxter on their last fishing trip.

A gentle breeze kept the mosquitos from buzzing around them as they settled into their watch. Without the boys' chatter, the sounds of the cicadas and frogs rose like an orchestra on the radio. Lightning bugs along the azalea bushes beyond the pond blinked to the rhythm.

Footsteps approached them on the flagstone path.

Ernest and Clive both turned. Ernest's mom came around the last lavender bush, two steaming mugs in her hands.

"Jo made y'all some tea. She'll be out later to check on you. Cyrus and I are going to see the little ones to bed. It looks like Baxter and Arabella will need extra soothing tonight."

"She's sensitive," Clive remarked as he accepted his cup.

"And caring. She's a beautiful soul. I just wish Sage had left her a bit of your mother's natural fire rather than absorbing all of it."

"It'll come to her," Clive remarked.

"It takes time and effort when it isn't inborn."

She handed Ernest his cup. Her smile made him wonder what she thought he was born with. Violence and a penchant for ruling others from his birth father?

"Do you need anything else right now, boys?"

"No thank you, Miss Fran." Clive took a sip of tea. "Good, it's not the relaxation one."

"She knows you promised Arabella and wouldn't sabotage your task. I'll see y'all later."

They drank in silence after she left.

Clive sat his empty cup on the blanket between them. "Do you think about how you might be like your old parents?"

"Yeah, especially when I'm being like my father."

"Why would you want to be like him?"

Ernest shrugged. "Getting a bit of respect instead of being teased or ignored."

"Did you respect your father or just fear him?"

"I don't need that shit talk from you, Clive." Ernest flung the rest of his tea into the pond and dropped the mug on the blanket. "You don't know what it's like to be constantly talked about because of your parents."

Clive laughed and Ernest's fists tightened.

"Yeah, I have no idea what it's like, Ernie. No one has ever called my mother a witch or asked if she aborts babies or sells love potions."

"But others accept you."

Clive leaned back on his elbows. "I'll never know if it's because they might fear retribution from my mother or want an in with her."

"So what do you do to find out if someone really likes you or is just using you?"

"Right now, I don't care." Clive paused, then whispered, "I think I hear something."

Ernest strained to listen as he studied the pond. The pointy muzzle of a fox nosed out of the azalea bush opposite the pond from them, whiskers quivering. It inched out of the shrubbery, then crept to the edge of the pond. Sitting upright, only its head moved back and forth as it watched the koi.

"It's the male," Clive whispered. "Sometimes it's the mother and her kits or all of them."

The sleek build coupled with the tawny fur with white patches was beautiful. Ernest knew Baxter would have loved seeing the fox this close except for those silly fish. One of the silvery ones was stupid enough to swim toward the predator.

"Ernie, clear them out of the way."

Ernest watched in fascination as the fox slowly raised a paw off the ground and rebalanced its rear weight. When the lone koi reached the striking area, Clive elbowed him hard.

Ernest sent the one at the edge swimming to the center of the pond, then herded the others there. The line of six fish would have been in perfect choreography if it weren't for the last two koi fighting against his control. Once there, he kept the fish toward the center of the pond, but wanted to see what else he could do. Controlling an adult human would be a lot different than fish—even a school of them—and he wasn't sure if Marie would expect that from him when he took the security job.

Rather than continue watching the fish, the fox raised its head and stared at Clive. Ernest had it tilt its head to the right, then stand, which it did wobbly at first. Then the stealthy omnivore rounded the pond toward the blanket.

"Ernie, what's it doing?"

Ernest chanced a quick look at Clive. Rather than a show of fear Ernest expected, Clive looked absent. Hearing the fox falter, Ernest refocused on the animal to keep it moving toward them.

When it was five feet away, hands went over Ernest's eyes from behind.

"Go on, get!" Jo said as she worked to keep her hands on Ernest's face as he struggled to free himself.

When the fox scuffled away, Clive got to his feet beside Ernest.

"Thanks for coming quickly, Mom."

"Go on inside, Clive. We'll be there soon."

"After you teach that showoff a lesson, I hope."

Ernest raised a middle finger in Clive's direction before he left. Once it was quiet, Jo released him to restore his vision.

"I've been proud of you until this moment, Ernest." Jo stood in front of him, eye to eye in the moonlight. "When Jim told me how you manipulated those fish in the bay, I only thought of the joy you gave your brother. But this—oh, Ernest! Leaping from fish to fox…You must know how immoral it is to control a living creature, especially if you're trying to scare someone with it."

"He deserved it."

"What has Clive ever—"

"He doesn't see me as an equal because I go to public school."

"I'm sure it's a misunderstanding. He considers you a friend, Ernest. He wouldn't purposely hurt your feelings." She took his hand. "Take deep breaths. Ground yourself."

"I'm not a little boy needing to be controlled."

"Everyone needs time to calm themselves and feel connected to the present." She blew out a breath perfumed with florals. "I'm not going to let go of you until I feel you relax."

It must have taken him at least ten minutes in the darkness with Jo literally breathing down his neck, but Ernest finally gained his freedom.

"Good, now I need your help." From her pocket, she pulled two small pouches fragrant with peppermint, garlic, and other things. "I mixed a repellent. We need to sprinkle it around the pond to keep predators away. Drop pinches of it about every foot. We'll start back-to-back and walk opposite ways around the water."

"Will it work?" Ernest asked after a few steps.

"Of course, but it needs to be reapplied every three days—more often if it rains heavily."

"Why didn't you tell Arabella you'd protect them with *your* magic?"

Jo looked at Ernest and smiled. "I wanted to be sure the koi were watched over until it was ready. Thank you for the time you put in."

"But no thanks for how it ended," he replied with a huff.

They were now a dozen feet away from each other and moving closer. When they were within touching distance, Jo held out her hand to collect the empty pouch and tucked it back into her pocket.

"I understand you need to test the limits, Ernest, but I wish you hadn't proven Jim right about everything he warned me against when he found out I was instructing you."

The weight of her words sat like a cannonball in his middle as he followed her to the house. Not wanting to see his mother, Ernest went right to the attic room he begrudgingly had to share with Clive all week.

Fourteen

Tuesday morning, Jim stood on Royal Street directing the flow of arriving visitors for the Mobile Chamber of Commerce's annual Buyers' Week. Automobiles and train riders from all over Southern Alabama, lower Mississippi, and the Florida panhandle were pouring into the city to shop and be entertained.

Registration traffic slowed slightly by the time Officer Murphy took over at noon so Jim could grab a lunch break. Knowing the restaurants downtown would be busy, Jim walked to the station to get his motorcycle before heading towards Our Alley.

Stu saw him park his bike at the curb and called out the window, "I'll have your regular in a minute, Officer Abbott!"

When Jim walked over, the handful of people in line waved him to the front.

"I appreciate it, y'all."

Stu handed out a glass of iced tea. "How's that crowd of shoppers doing?"

"They rolled in like a bank of thunderheads on an August afternoon and are ready to light the town." Jim swallowed some tea. "How are things down here?"

"Wild. I think those boys know the extra officers are busy. Two shops down the road had to chase gangs away that were harassing customers, and our regular table waifs are hiding. Don't bother to leave food. It'll just go to the yellowjackets."

"I'll eat quick and then patrol." Jim checked his wristwatch. "I should be able to stay in the area for about an hour."

"Good. Them boys need the reminder they ain't gonna get away with things." Stu slid Jim's plate out the window. "And that lady friend of yours was down here earlier."

Jim paused, hand on his plate. "Was she asking for me?"

"Nope. I guess she decided she liked herself a younger man instead." Stu's teeth were bright amid his dark face. "She was chatting up the one with curly hair and mean glare. She must have been doing a good job of things because he actually grinned a few times."

"She was talking to Ryan?"

Stu nodded. "Don't be jealous, officer, or you'll ruin that story about her only needing police help."

Frowning, Jim took a seat. He thought Stu might have exaggerated about the neighborhood kids not watching for scraps, but no eyes peered out from the fence slats. The boys had to be doing more than heckling customers for the children to miss out.

Jim was down to his last piece of fried chicken when yelling came from the next block. He was on his feet when shouts filled the air, running for the nearest alley.

Stu's lanky stride passed him at the corner. "That sounds like my brother!"

Following Stu's lead, Jim came upon a group of a dozen white teens circling like vultures in a barren courtyard. Stu tried to bust through their ranks, but the boys linked arms and crowded him out.

"Break it up!" Jim commanded as he took the nearest boy's shoulders and tugged him back.

"It's a cop!" The boy shirked Jim's hands and ran, causing a frenzy of activity that included five others jumping Stu, who had reached the kid in the middle.

"Cut it out!" Jim shoved through the stragglers to reach Stu. "Y'all are gonna get hauled to the station for disorderly conduct if you don't stop!"

Jim grabbed the fleshy arm of one of the boys swinging at Stu and yanked him back. "Scotty, you should be ashamed of yourself."

Once Jim had the biggest one out of the picture, the others scattered.

"Sit your ass against the wall, Scotty, and tell your friends to do the same." Jim nudged him to the side.

Stu cradled his brother, rocking him as he groaned.

"Try not to move him too much, Stu," Jim said as he took a moment to look them over, to be sure the boy was breathing. "You don't know what injuries he might have."

Jim turned his full attention on Scotty and his remaining friends. "There's nothing you can prove by beating a kid. What got into y'all?"

Scotty met Jim's gaze. "Ryan's parting order was that whoever gave the best beating today was the new leader."

Stu looked up, dark eyes filled with anguish that switched to hatred as sudden as a strike of lightning. "You goddamn bastards!"

Before Jim could get between them, Stu had Scotty on the ground. He pummeled his face, cursing him every which way for beating his little brother.

Jim pulled Stu back and got in front of his heaving form. "I know you're mad, Stu, but I don't want to have to drag you to the station too. Your brother's gonna need you, ya hear?"

Once Scotty was on his feet, Jim held onto his arm in-part to steady him, but also to keep him angled away so his dripping nose wouldn't get blood on his uniform. "You look worse than that kid, Scotty. I think that means Stu's in charge of this area now."

A couple of the boys snickered, but most sneered.

"Like hell a n—" one of the boys started to say.

"Y'all better stop before things go too far," Jim said, cutting him off sharply. "Now clear on out and forget the idea of ruling things in these parts, unless you want to take a trip to the police station with Scotty."

The others ran as the regular policeman for the neighborhood arrived. Jim updated Officer Keegan, who asked a neighbor to send for a Negro doctor before going to the nearest callbox to request the transport wagon.

By the time Jim made it back to Royal Street, it was half past two—just in time to get word from one of the Chamber of Commerce delegates for him to escort a procession of two hundred Buyers' Week visitors to Hartwell Field. Frustration over the senseless violence had Jim wanting to rev the engine and drive as fast as he could until he hit the country roads north of town where he'd ride until he ran out of gas. Instead, he was stuck leading the line of buses and automobiles down Government to Ann Street at the top speed of five miles per hour.

During the baseball game, Jim leaned against the wall outside the stadium, arms across his chest. The *thwack* of the bats striking the baseball and the cheers of the crowd kept him from dozing off though his body yearned for a nap. Going to bed early the night before had only afforded him more time to toss and turn. Since they were married, he had never slept without Francesca, save for the days he grabbed a few hours of sleep when he was scheduled on nightshift. But even then, Francesca was in the house. He ached for her comforting presence.

One of the stadium attendants brought Jim a lemonade and bag of popcorn. He thanked the man and perched on a bench near the exit to enjoy the last few innings of the game.

Down an exit aisle, the glint of sun off bright hair caught his eye. Marie walked purposely into the shade of the tunneled path, a white fan flickering in front of her glistening face. Her eyes were on whoever was approaching her. With a smile, she held out a small piece of paper and started walking. Jim shifted far enough on the bench to witness Marie hand the note to Ryan on her way to the exit. He slipped the paper into a pocket and turned for the bleachers opposite Jim. Uneasiness squirmed inside Jim as he remembered Ryan saying he was moving on, and Scotty's remarks about new leadership. If a hardened soul like Ryan was going to be working for Capone, Jim was glad he was making an effort to separate Ernest from Marie's schemes.

The Mobile Bears beat Little Rock, and Jim escorted the Buyers' Week group back to town. He checked in at the station, hoping to go home for the day.

"Abbott," a lieutenant called. "Are you done with the Hartwell Field detail?"

"Yes, sir."

"Grab something to eat next door at Morrison's, then we need you for another job. Would you rather direct traffic down Dauphin near the theaters or at the arena at Royal and Canal for the boxing tournament?"

"Boxing because the men won't care if I'm a tad gruff. It's been a long day, and I don't have it in me for banter and smiles."

"Muster up a bit of friendliness, Abbott. The spectators might not care, but the Chamber biggies will." The lieutenant slapped his back as he passed him. "But the chief is pleased with your arrest of that teen this afternoon. If crime rates drop on that side, we'll have you to thank."

After eating, Jim drove his motorcycle more than half a dozen blocks to the arena. The sponsor of the boxing tournament, the American Legion Athletic Association, had plenty of volunteers around the place. Jim stood on the corner to watch the roads until the traffic increase merited a bit of help.

While the rounds were being played and with the traffic at a lower volume, Jim stepped into the smoky establishment to enjoy a cigarette of his own and take in a few fights amid the shouting and boisterousness. Far from being restful, it nonetheless allowed him to unwind before he needed to direct the exiting crowd.

He returned his motorcycle to the station and took the streetcar toward Washington Square at midnight. At home, Jim fed the cats and freshened their water dishes. A simple sandwich with the remainder of the cold cuts and cheese quieted his stomach, but a shower did little to revive him. Jim settled on the double bed, breathing in the floral scent that clung to Francesca's pillow as he drifted to sleep.

On Wednesday, he performed the same daytime duties.

When Jim led the baseball watchers back downtown, he noticed Ryan leaning against the Methodist church at the corner of Broad Street. Wishing he could circle back to check on him, Jim was forced to report in at the station.

"You look as welcoming as horse shit, Abbott. Long days in the heat will do that to a man."

"Yes, sir." Jim guzzled his cup of water, hoping it would cure his headache.

"Take three hours, but I need you back to direct traffic for that bathing beauty contest at the Saenger tonight. Thursday evening won't be so bad with many of the folks taking that excursion across the bay. I'll try to let you off early tomorrow."

"Thank you, Lieutenant. I'll see you tonight."

Jim took the streetcar west. As he approached home, Jack ran towards him at the Church Street corner.

"Where's Ernie, Officer Abbott?" He asked as he tossed the baseball to him. "Everyone's asking about him."

Jim barely managed to catch it. "His mother took the boys out of town for a bit. They'll return this weekend." He tossed it back.

"I wish he would have told me and Theo goodbye."

"It was a last-minute plan." Jim went for the front steps.

"I guess. He didn't tell Miss Marley he was leaving either."

Jim turned so fast, he almost fell over. "Miss Marley what?"

"She asked if I'd seen him."

"Why?"

Jack's eyes widened, then he licked his lips nervously and shrugged. "They've been talkin' lately. Theo asked after him too."

Inside, Jim asked the telephone operator for Jo's house as he removed his jacket. When the housekeeper answered, he asked Sarah for Francesca.

"She's on the veranda, Officer Abbott. It'll be a minute."

"Hello, Jim?" Francesca's voice was tight with worry.

"Is everything all right, baby?"

"I hope so, but Ernest…" Even with the Harringtons' private line, they couldn't say much on the telephone when the operators might be listening. "He had a falling out with Clive the first night, and they haven't made up yet."

"Do I need to come out and talk to him?"

"No, you need your rest. Jo, Cyrus, and I have spoken with them. It'll just take more time than we expected."

"All right, baby. And he hasn't talked to anyone on the telephone?"

"No one," Francesca assured him. "Jo even asks the operator twice a day if there have been any ingoing or outgoing calls."

"Good." Jim sighed. "Telephone if you change your mind about he talking to him. I've got a few hours right now, but I'm directing traffic tonight."

"I will, Jim. I love you."

He returned her love and hung the receiver. The bottle of milk from the morning delivery was his dinner. Then Jim showered, set his alarm, and dropped into bed. Sunny slept at his feet, but Rochester sat watch at the bedroom door as though waiting for his mistress to return.

***

Jim stood in the middle of Dauphin Street at nine that night, stopping the one-way traffic so a couple dozen pedestrians could cross toward Joachim Street on their way to the theater. Along with the headache still lingering from earlier in the day, a wave of nausea swept him. Holding his breath several seconds, he slowly released it as he lowered his arm and followed the last person to the sidewalk.

Veering a block west, Jim stepped behind the Saenger as he began trembling. He clutched the rim of the first trashcan and spewed the sweet tea he had drunk when he arrived at the station for night duty. After a brief pause, the other meager contents of his stomach painted the metal can too.

With a groan, Jim fell to his knees. His vision blurred before he blacked out.

"Abbott!"

He felt rushing air before his face.

"Come on, Abbott. You need to wake up before the lieutenant slaps you in the hospital."

Jim cracked his eyes and found Officer Murphy fanning him with a hat while Officer Green looked on.

"There ya are, old boy." Officer Murphy grinned with relief and set his hat back on his head. "Let's get you sitting up, then Green will give you some water."

"What happened?" Jim asked as Murphy tugged him upright and leaned him against the brick wall.

"From the look and smell of things," Green said as he handed over a glass, "I'd say you got sick and passed out. Don't tell me you were drinking on the clock."

Jim clutched the smooth glass, hoping to keep a grip on it though he could barely lift it.

"It's the heat, I'll bet." Murphy frowned as he undid Jim's bowtie, released the top button of the shirt, and opened his jacket for him. "One of the perils of our job in summer."

"Good thing I saw you cut down the alley a while back," Officer Green said. "When you didn't turn up after the beauty contest let out, I knew where to start looking for you."

"What time is it?"

"Quarter after eleven." Murphy picked up Jim's hat from the ground and brushed it off. He pointed at the glass of water Jim was still holding. "Be sure to drink it all. Green here went to the trouble of getting it and needs to return the glass before the restaurant tracks him down."

Jim chugged the rest of it.

"Damn, Abbott! Where's your head today?" Murphy asked. "You gotta drink it slow."

"Ernest," Jim mumbled. "And—"

Officer Green saved the glass before it fell from Jim's grasp as he retched. "I'll be back with another one."

Half an hour later, Jim was on his feet, though shaky. The second glass of water seemed to slosh inside him with each step. Officers Murphy and Green walked on either side of Jim as they slowly made their way east on Conti Street.

"Once we get to the station," Murphy said, "I'll call a cab and see you home."

"You'd make a swell date, Abbott. You can't even stay upright." Green snickered.

"He can't help it if he's dainty in his old age," Murphy said, trying to hide a smile.

"Y'all better be glad I'm useless right now or you'd be on your asses in a heartbeat."

"Hear that, Happy? He thinks he can whup us at the same time." Green continued ribbing Jim, making the tedious three-block journey seem a little quicker.

At the police station, the shift lieutenant checked over Jim and forced him to drink another glass of water while they waited for the transport wagon to come—Jim's free taxi for the night.

"Sleep as much as you need to, Abbott," the lieutenant said. "As long as you can get here by noon, that is."

Officer Green helped Murphy get Jim into the back of the transport wagon and said goodbye.

"You don't need to come with me, Happy," Jim told Officer Murphy once he was sitting on the bench.

"I'll see you to your wife, Abbott."

"Fran isn't home." Jim leaned his head back on the wall as they started moving. "She's out in Spring Hill with the boys for the week."

"Don't you have enough sense to eat and drink to stay fit without a wife looking after you?" His tone was joking, but there was an edge of concern in it.

"It's too damn hot to want to eat, and I've had a lot on my mind lately."

Officer Murphy escorted Jim into the house, setting him at the kitchen table with a spotted banana and another glass of water. "If you look like hell in the morning, stay put. I'll vouch for ya."

"Thanks, Happy."

Jim was glad he had seen to the cats earlier in the evening so he didn't have to deal with their food. Sunny meowed and circled his legs as he drank, while Rochester kept watch from the doorway to the back porch. Jim peeled the banana. The scent of its over-ripeness gagged him, but he managed to slowly eat.

Walking with one hand on the wall to reach the bathroom, he left his uniform and accessories in a heap and nearly tripped stepping into the bathtub. A filled tub was too dangerous in his state, so Jim showered in the tap water that came out of the pipes as hot as the air. He dry-heaved several times, but fortunately didn't lose anything.

After a hasty toweling, he dragged himself to his room. Jim pulled on a pair of underdrawers and collapsed on the bed. He watched the ceiling fan whirl until darkness took him once more.

Too tired to move, his sleep was nonetheless restless. Jim let himself drift, falling through memories. Dancing with Francesca in her parlor in preparation for a salon at Mathias and Cordelia's house. The glow of pride when Francesca saw him for the first time on his motorcycle. Her shining face on Ernest's adoption day. Ernest holding his baby brother… How much time passed during his stupor he didn't know.

The touch of a hand on Jim's clammy cheek soothed him before dawn, but when his eyes flickered open, no one was there. The lingering woodsy scent, like rosemary and pine, made him think it would be easy to slip into eternal darkness with the hint of the outdoors around him.

***

Jim woke at the sensation of being watched. When the figure of someone standing at his bedside came into view, he flinched, reaching for his sidearm that wasn't there.

162

"I'm sorry to startle you, Jim." Deborah Farley's voice was gentle. "If I had known you would wake this time, I would have announced myself."

"This time?" Jim fingered the sheet that covered him and glanced around the room. His holster was on top of the dresser beside his hat and wristwatch though he knew he'd left everything in the bathroom before he went to bed.

"I've been here since daylight." Her warm hand rested on his ashen face. "Josephine checked on you during her midnight wanderings. When she saw how pale and listless you were, she asked me to watch over you while she brews a special tea."

"Thanks, Deborah. I appreciate the help."

She smiled, eyes crinkling at the corners. "All right, Jim. Get yourself to the bathroom."

His face heated. "I don't need to go, but you'll need to leave when I do get out of bed."

"I already saw your striped boxer shorts when I covered you with the sheet."

Jim laughed, but a sharp pain split his head. He winced and closed his eyes.

"I'll bring you a bowl of bone broth. You can have as much of that as you'd like until Josephine comes."

"I don't need one of Jo's potions." Jim sat up and swung his legs over the side of the bed to try to prove his point. The result was a dizzying sensation and the bedroom going topsy-turvy, which caused him to fall onto his side.

"Must you be so stubborn? I'm trying to make this easier on you." Deborah sat beside him. Once he heaved himself upright, she leaned into his side to support him. "What was the last thing you ate?"

"A banana around midnight."

"And before that?"

Jim started to shrug, but it took too much effort. "What day is it?"

"Thursday." Deborah's arm went around his back. "Your skin is as parched as your aura. What have you been eating and drinking the last two days?"

"The restaurants are over-crowded right now."

"I know you have more sense than to go without while you're working, and you're always welcome at my house, Jim."

"I had milk and sweet tea yesterday, not to mention some water."

"*Some?* You need that most. Sweet tea isn't the best refreshment in the heat. And then you ate nothing on top of that?" She shook her head like an unhappy mother though she was only a few years older than Jim. "And to think you were balanced not even two weeks ago."

"I've been at wit's end since I've witnessed Ernest carelessly using his abilities. And then the whole thing with Marie. Plus she's in contact with another young man who I don't want influencing my son, either."

"Try not to worry about Ernest right now. Josephine is keeping him safe." Deborah stood, fluffed the pillows against the headboard, and helped him sit upright against them. "I'll be back in a minute."

Jim sighed as he allowed himself to sink fully into the pillows. He tried to relax, but the thought of Jo's astral visit conjured all sorts of disturbing ideas. A glance at his alarm clock showed it was nine-ten. He'd have time to eat, then drive out to Spring Hill before reporting to the station.

Deborah brought him a tray with a bowl of broth, a glass of water, and two buttered slices of her homemade wheat bread. She waited quietly to see that he could handle everything without assistance before withdrawing. Soon, the comforting sounds of domesticity in the form of dishes being put away and humming made their way down the hall.

When Deborah returned, Jim spoke from the heart. "I hope Alvin knows how lucky he is."

"Of course he does." Deborah blushed and took the tray from him. "You can nap until Josephine arrives."

"I need to get to Jo's house this morning before I report to work."

"This morning?" Deborah's brows rose.

Jim motioned to the clock, realizing it still said ten after nine because he'd forgotten to wind it the day before. "What time is it?"

"Nearly four in the afternoon."

"I was supposed to report no later than noon! The chief will terminate me as soon as I show my face at the station." Jim scrambled to the edge of the bed, trying to ignore the wave of dizziness it produced.

Deborah placed a hand on his shoulder to keep him seated. "You're not going anywhere today, Jim. Especially not before Josephine administers her tea."

"But I'm missing one of the busiest days of the year!"

"I telephoned the station after I arrived, informing them I had dropped by and found you unconscious with a fever, which isn't far from the truth. They know you've had two long days in the heat. Rest, Jim. Don't fret over what you can't control."

"Which is everything, apparently." He fell back on the pillows.

"I know you value helping and maintaining order, but that's impossible to do every moment of the day, as your aura and physical health can attest." She collected his tray. "Try to sleep, Jim. I'll wake you in another hour to drink more if Josephine hasn't arrived by then."

Fifteen

Bored after having leafed through the daily newspaper for
the second time that day, Ernest pulled himself up from the
sofa. If he was in town, he'd be out with Jack and Theodore,
playing ball and cutting up. Not to mention eating hot dogs or
something else good. The thought made is stomach rumble.
He was hungry enough to brave the strong odor wafting from
kitchen compliments of the tea Miss Jo had been simmering all
day.

"Dinner will be another fifteen minutes," Miss Sarah said
from the stove.

She wiped her hands on her apron and looked around
before waving him over. Ernest followed her to a far cabinet,
where she pulled a red tin of butter cookies out. "Grab a
couple before Jo returns."

"Thanks, Miss Sarah!"

He took four of the golden treats and shoved one into his
mouth. After three days of no food with animal products
except seafood, it tasted as joyful as Christmas.

"I keep them on hand for Cyrus," she whispered
conspiratorially. "I've shared a few with your mother this week,

but you don't tend to come in unless you're clearing the table with the others."

"I didn't know what I was missing out on."

"Jo is showering, so she'll be a few more minutes. Could you ask Cyrus to call the others inside to wash up?"

Ernest popped another cookie in his mouth and nodded.

When Cyrus went through the library to call the others inside, Ernest hastily picked up the telephone and asked the operator for the Marley house on Roper Street.

"Hello?"

"Miss—"

"Ernie? Where have you been?"

"Out at the Harringtons' in Spring Hill. My parents didn't give me a choice."

"Do you still want the job?"

"Yes, ma'am. I really need it." Through the French doors, Ernest saw Cyrus approaching the house. "I have to go now."

"Meet me where the Harringtons' driveway intersects the main road in an hour. I'll wait for fifteen minutes, but if you don't make it, you'll have to contact me when I'm back in town to schedule something else."

The line went dead before Ernest could reply.

He hung the receiver and wiped his sweaty hands on the thighs of his jeans as he stepped away. Cyrus breezed in from the veranda.

"You better get to the nearest bathroom if you don't want to stand in line to washup," Cyrus warned, his square jaw firm though a smile turned up his cheeks.

"Yes, sir." Ernest hurried to the half-bath under the stairs.

When his face and hands were scrubbed, Ernest passed the Harrington girls in the hall. He looked in the formal dining room and noticed there were two fewer place settings than normal.

"What's going on?" he asked when he found Miss Jo and his mother filling jars of the brown brew at the long kitchen counter.

His mom stepped toward him. "Miss Jo and I are going into town for a little bit."

"Why? Who's all that for?"

She pressed her lips together and tucked her hair behind her ear. "Jim. He's under the weather."

"Jim never gets sick except in the winter every couple of years."

"I know. I'm worried too. Apparently heat exhaustion struck him last night. Jo's going to drop me off along with the tea." She hugged Ernest. "And before you ask, you can't ride along. I need you to help Cyrus watch Baxter and the others, all right?"

Ernest nodded against the shoulder of her green dress.

"Could I help y'all carry the baskets to the automobile? His mom's arms tightened around his shoulders and he leaned into her, wishing for a moment he was still small enough to curl up in her lap. Those first months Ernest was with Miss Fran, all it took was a hug to know he was loved. Now his thoughts tried to shame him. How good of a son was he when he was planning to run away to work for Marie? Would Louisa even like him if he had fancy clothes and money to spend on her?

Ernest felt his mother intake a shaky breath. He straightened and saw her eyes were red-rimmed. "Mom?"

She forced a smile and dabbed the back of her hand against a cheek as though feeling for tears. "I'm worried about Jim."

The clinking sound of the jars tapping into one another as Miss Jo loaded the lidded concoction into a basket pulled his attention.

"Could I at least help y'all by carrying the basket to the automobile?"

"Sure, Ernest." His mom kissed his forehead. "That would be great. And I'll telephone first thing in the morning to give you an update."

Dinner—another fish, rice, and vegetable meal—had Ernest checking the mantel clock every few minutes. Without his mother and Miss Jo there to chatter, everyone ate quicker than usual. Ernest offered to clear the table so the little ones could go up for baths.

"Want any help?" Clive asked.

"No thanks. I'm used to daily chores. Most lowly public-school kids have to do them, ya know."

Clive smirked. "I guess I sounded like a heel the other day. I'm sorry."

Ernest shrugged. "You can't help it if you think playing in the dirt is more fun than baseball."

"We're okay now, right?"

"I guess, just don't ask me to mist your ferns ever again."

Laughing, Clive nodded. "Fair enough. Tell my dad I went up to the attic to check my plant in the windowsill."

"Sure."

Ernest cleared the table, then put on his socks and shoes that were tucked in the entry hall.

As he reached for the doorknob, a soft voice spoke. "We're not supposed to go outside."

Arabella stood at the base of the stairs like a miniature version of her mother with the same bobbed hair and piercing hazel eyes.

"I'm going to the porch for a moment. I want to see if the stars will be out tonight or if it's cloudy."

"The stars are always there, clouds or not."

"Well, yeah." Her uncanny gaze made his hands sweat. "Where's Baxter?"

"Getting his bath. My daddy sent me to tell you that you can use the shower next."

"Thanks, Arabella. I'll be up in a minute." He turned back to the door.

"We aren't allowed to go outside tonight."

Frustration over the blockade of his only chance to escape erupted as he returned her stare. "You can play by the rules, Arabella, but I make my own."

"The rules are for everyone."

Glaring at her, he only saw her mother who had kept watch over him like a jailer the past several days. Arabella's freckled face changed from righteous passivity to fear as her eyes widened. Only when her upper arms began to press into her torso did Ernest realize he was mentally squeezing her.

"Don't tell anyone you saw me," he commanded as he loosened his hold.

A single tear rolled down her cheek.

"Promise me, Arabella."

She shook her head. "Baxter never told me you were bad."

Blinded by frustration over losing his temper, Ernest dropped his control. Arabella sank to the floor in tears. Rather than apologize, he ran outside in an attempt to escape his guilt.

Ernest sprinted down the driveway toward Old Shell Road. As he passed an automobile that was parked along the tree line, it roared to life.

"Ernie! Ernie, wait!" Marie pulled next to him. "Get in the backseat."

Yanking the door open, he fell into the shadowed space. "Go. She might have told someone by now. It won't take long before they see I'm missing."

"You're fine now, Ernie." Marie turned west, heading further away from Mobile.

"Not if he's scared of getting caught after escaping a witch's house," a sardonic voice sounded from the passenger seat.

With the automobile dark and his distraction, Ernest hadn't looked anywhere but to Marie. The guy sitting beside her had raven curls and an icy glare when he turned around.

"Ernie, this is Ryan," Marie said as they rumbled down the country road. "He's new this week as well."

"You don't look like much," Ryan said.

"Neither do you." Ernest guessed he was about nineteen, but the hardness in his eyes made him seem older.

Ryan laughed. "You've got pluck, I'll give you that much, but you gotta get over being scared of anyone, even a witch."

"I doubt Josephine will be coming home anytime soon," Marie remarked.

"Why do you say that?" Ernest asked.

"Word around Washington Square is that your father is bed-ridden. Deborah Farley has been nursing him all day, waiting for a cure to be delivered by Witchy Wolf, as she used to be called. Something happened to him while on duty last night. The police transport wagon had to bring him home."

"Duty? Police?" Ryan turned to stare at Ernest. "Don't tell me your old man is a cop!"

"I didn't mention that to you?" Marie asked. "Ernie's dad is Officer Abbott of the Flying Squadron."

"That blowhard? I've pushed him around a few times. Now I'm really not impressed with you, kid. Why are you letting this tyke join you, Marie?"

"Ernie has a very particular set of skills that will give us the upper hand over anyone."

"Even the police or the feds?"

"*Anyone.* Ernie is extremely gifted."

Ryan snorted. "That's what they say about my cousin, but she's eleven and eats paste."

"Trust me, Ryan." Marie's hand touched his cheek when she glanced from the road to him. "Play nice and stay on Ernie's good side."

Ryan cut another deadly look at Ernest before shifting closer to Marie and turning fully to the front.

As the miles rolled by, Ernest tried to relax into the leather seat but something about the way Marie acted turned him sour. Maybe it was the way she had touched Ryan's cheek or made light of Jim's sickness. Ernest wasn't sure if he still wanted to work for her, but if Jim died, what would his mom and Baxter do? Surely Miss Jo would take them in, or the judge set her up in one of his apartments, but would she accept any of that? His mother was proud in her way, always wanting to wear the prettiest dresses and have the tidiest yard on the street. If Marie was truthful about the money he would earn watching over Commissioner Beauchamp's house, Ernest would need the job more than ever so he could send an allowance to his mother, though he still wanted to build his status in the eyes of Louisa.

When Marie finally slowed the automobile to turn between two stately gate posts, Ernest stiffened. She parked in the circular driveway with a fountain in the center across from an impressive house.

"Richard and my sister are living here this summer, but they're across the bay with their children and my mother for the week. You'll meet him when they return. By then Ryan should be installed in the household on the backlot, but Ernest will be staying in the helps' cottage."

Ernest followed them inside, glad he wouldn't have to room with Ryan. He shivered when the artificially cold air met his skin.

"Get comfortable, boys. I'll be right back."

"I don't like being grouped with a kid," Ryan called after her. Seeing that she ignored him and passed through a doorway on the left side of the curving staircase, he huffed and stepped into the living room with Ernest.

Only a side table lamp was on in the cavernous space. Ernest eyed the arched fireplace and wood-trimmed walls as he took a seat on the plush sofa.

Ryan threw himself into the nearest armchair, and Marie re-joined them carrying a tray with three wine goblets.

"You're joining us as a man, Ernie. We'll not pander to you." She stared at the other boy. "Will we, Ryan?"

Ryan shrugged and snatched a goblet.

Ernest took one, then Marie set the tray on the coffee table and lifted the final glass for herself.

"To new beginnings."

Ernest inhaled the fruity aroma with interest, but his sip tasted like old socks, making his mouth pucker. Ryan's face didn't look much better.

"At least there's something you both agree on. I'll find something more to your liking later," Marie said. "But for now, do either of you have questions?"

Ernest set down his wine. "What exactly is Commissioner Beauchamp's business here? It just looks like a house."

"It's better if you don't know the details."

"I thought we weren't pandering to him," Ryan said with a smirk.

Marie flashed an annoyed look at him before smiling at Ernest. "The acreage out here is a place for pleasure and entertainment. This house is only a fraction of all there is to offer."

"I thought your brother-in-law was in politics."

"He is, Ernie, but Richard manages the gaming den in the basement. I'm his assistant, overseeing things on the whole property when he can't be here because of his position in the city." She took another drink and placed her glass next to Ernest's. "The men in charge of security are ready to get back to town before they're sent to Florida for the winter. I was tasked with hiring some new blood to be trained in the meantime."

"That's my job. I get to beat the men who don't follow the rules in the other house." Ryan cracked his knuckles. "I've got a lot of practice fighting, so don't try me, kid."

"You're not as tough as me."

"I could beat you and your old man at the same time."

Ernest mentally fisted Ryan's shirt at the chest and hauled him upright.

"Hey!" Fear flashed across his face as he looked around in alarm. When his gaze fell on Ernest, it narrowed.

"Ernie," Marie said in an even tone, "I don't allow my men to fight amongst themselves."

"No one's fighting, Miss Marie." Ernest dropped Ryan back in his chair, unable to hide the smile of satisfaction it gave him.

"Good." Marie crossed her legs. "But that's just what I need from your services, tossing around grown men when needed. You see a threat and you deal with it without overthinking. You're perfect." She looked at Ryan to drive her point home. "In another few years, you might be taking orders from Ernie."

When he snorted, she continued.

"You've seen what Ernest can do. He's all I'll need out here. If you don't like someone four years your junior showing you up, you can find your way back to the city to play mayor to that group of misfits I rescued you from."

Ryan crossed his arms, scowling, but didn't reply.

Marie laughed. "I don't think he likes that idea, Ernie, but let's give him time to get used to it. Ryan, I'll bring you over to the back house and introduce you to Orson and the girls. You can stay here and rest, Ernie, though you'll have to get used to staying up all night."

Ernest nodded, but refused to meet Ryan's glare. Marie went to a wall-mounted telephone box just beyond the doorway and lifted the receiver.

"We made it back, Orson. I told you there was nothing to worry about. I'm bringing Ryan over to say hello, but I want him staying here the first few nights."

Marie bid Ernest to relax as she and Ryan departed.

Once he was alone, Ernest tried to sit on the sofa, but his skin was prickling with energy. He was glad to have given Ryan a taste of what he was capable of, but he still wasn't comfortable about the idea of working with him even if he'd be in a different building.

A clock in the next room chimed the hour as though signally his time was running out.

Ernest thought if he left now, he could walk up to one of the main roads and hitchhike back to town. He wanted to know how Jim was and be sure his mother and Baxter were all right.

Ernest went to the front door and opened it. Along with the humid air that rushed in, dread at seeing the huge figure of a suited man standing near the automobile made him shiver.

"Well, that's done with," Marie said as she waltzed into the hall from the back of the house. "What are you doing at the door?"

Ernest closed it. "I—I thought I heard something. There's a man out there."

"That's Orson, making his rounds." Marie clicked the lock on the front door. "He's always about, checking on things. He's armed but also skilled in physical means of suppression."

"Where's Ryan?" Ernest asked as Marie led him to the sofa.

"Enjoying a hearty welcome from one of the girls." Marie took the seat beside Ernest. "And how are you settling in?"

"All right, thanks. But I wish I'd had the time to pack before leaving," he said in hopes of her offering to take him by his house the next day.

"We can make a list and send a man into town to purchase what you need. Do you know your clothing sizes?"

He nodded. "I was just fitted for new pants and shirts last month."

"That's terrific. I had hoped you would be all right with everything that happened today, especially after hearing about Jim."

Ernest shrugged off the sensation of despair at the continued references to his father, but he'd use it if it meant giving him more time to figure a way out of his situation. "He's been on my case too much. He'll never understand my need to do something more."

"I'm glad you accepted the position, Ernie. Everything will be fine from here on out."

Sixteen

Jim lay propped on the pillows in his bed at home, Francesca curled at his side, holding his hand. Jo was in the kitchen, heating another serving of her special tea before returning to Spring Hill for the night. Having to drink the brew warm to aid digestion wasn't ideal when Jim craved a tall glass of iced tea, but he couldn't deny he felt stronger than he had since the night before.

A knock sounded on the front door causing Francesca to shift in preparation for standing.

"Stay with me, baby." Jim whispered. "Jo can get it."

Francesca's smile was laced with concern, but he was pleased worry no longer painted her face.

"What are you doing here at this hour, Sean?" Jo's pointed voice asked.

"I could ask the same of you, Josephine, especially since I heard Francesca isn't home."

"Jim's like a little brother to me, as you well know. Besides that, your rumor mill has a broken gear because Fran is here too. Come in. You can help me deliver Jim's tea."

"Potion, more like it."

As their voices drew closer, Francesca sat up and smoothed her emerald dress around her legs.

A moment later, Jo was at their bedside, handing Jim a canning jar wrapped in a cloth so he wouldn't have to touch the hot glass. "You have a visitor."

"So I heard." Jim nodded his thanks to Jo and looked at his guest standing in his doorway. "Come in, Judge Spunner. What brings you here tonight?"

"I came to find out for myself which, if any, of the rumors were true." He stopped at the foot of the bed.

"And how do they stack up?" Jim drank from the glass as he waited for what was sure to be a colorful reply.

"The one about Francesca not being here is proved false since I see the lovely vision of her beside you." The judge winked at her. "But I was told Francesca took the boys and left because you'd been stepping out on her. And that you were being nursed by Deborah—probably innocently, but possibly not—after you were attacked in a downtown alley last night by a gang of teens. They beat you, and I heard both that it involved knife wounds, but also it was out-of-state mobsters who shot you. But in either case, you were left for dead and the guilty parties stole your motorcycle."

Jim grinned. "Those stories are a heap more exciting than what actually happened."

"Which was…"

"Heat exhaustion due to stubborn negligence," Francesca said as she stood. "Please stop talking and drink, Jim."

"He's been concerned about Ernest and overworked," Jo continued as Francesca's focus was on Jim as he lifted the jar to his lips. "He neglected himself and took ill, passing out behind the Saenger when he should have been directing traffic."

"But why wasn't Francesca here?"

"She brought the boys to my house," Jo continued, "so I could help keep an eye on Ernest while Jim was busy with Buyers' Week events."

"Why?"

"Because Ernest needs to be kept away from Marie Marley," Francesca declared.

"Marie?"

"She knows about his telekinesis and wants to utilize his power." Francesca placed a hand on the judge's arm. "Now if you will excuse us, Jim needs his rest. Maybe Jo can see you out when she leaves."

"But what's the darling up to?"

Jim swallowed the rest of the tea and set the jar on the side table. "She's Capone's darling now, working with Commissioner Beauchamp in their den of debauchery at his country estate. As I mentioned to you the other week, you needed to stay away from the parties out there."

The judge's brow rose, a look of amusement on his face. "Fancy that! And Marie was such a quiet girl, hiding behind the piano in her youth."

"Enough with the reminiscing, Sean." Francesca nudged his arm. "It's time for you to say goodnight."

"But there's so much to learn yet!"

Jo laughed. "True, but there's always tomorrow. If you don't leave, I'll toss your spirit so far out of Mobile you won't be able to find your way back before Christmas."

"You couldn't do anything of the sort," the judge retorted.

"Try me, Sean Spunner. I dare you."

"You damn witch."

"When it suits my purposes, yes. And I'm back on my old turf, defending my friends. If you're ready to try yourself against Witchy Wolf of Washington Square, I'll slip you a potion that will make you impotent for life."

The judge scoffed at Jo's brazenness, then turned to Jim still propped on the pillows. "I'm glad you're on the mend. Josephine is a handy woman to have around, as long as you're on the same side."

"Yes, and thank you for your concern. And you, Jo, for everything." Jim added. "Cyrus will have expected you home by now. Not to mention Fran and I need your eyes on Ernest."

"All ri—" Jo's gaze shifted heavenward, her focus on an unseen point, body frozen.

A smile of wonder shone on Judge Spunner's face as he watched Jo, as spellbound as she appeared to be herself.

"Ernest is gone," Jo said as she snapped out of her trance.

"How?" Francesca asked as Jim sat up.

"He slipped out after dinner. Arabella tried to stop him, but he mentally restrained her. When Sage heard what happened, she astral projected to locate him. Ernest was heading west in an automobile driven by a blonde." She looked at Jim. "You've only had three doses. I'm not sure if you're well enough to go with me."

"You're not going without me." Jim put his legs over the side of the bed in preparation of standing as Jo silently measured him. She gave a nod of approval. "You know where we're headed. We'll use your truck."

"And me?" Francesca asked.

"No, Fran. Not for this. Sean, I need you to bring Fran to Deborah's house. I'll be able to telepathically send word to Deborah, and Fran will have company while she waits."

"I'd be glad to help."

"If you could give me and Fran a minute," Jim told the others, "I'll be ready soon."

Jo closed the bedroom door behind her and the judge.

Wasting no time, Jim stood to hug his wife, breathing in her essence as he waited for his lightheadedness to pass. "I love you, Francesca. Try not to worry too much. Between me and Jo, we'll bring Ernest home."

Her warm hands trailed his back, infusing him with her vivacity as he expanded his aura to embrace her spirit. "I don't want to lose any of you."

"You won't." He kissed her to seal his pledge then went to the closet for clothing.

"Will you wear your uniform?"

"Baby, it's out of my jurisdiction. And I'm going to him as his father, not a policeman, though I'll carry my gun and badge." Jim pulled on a summer-weight navy suit.

"You look a little pale, Jim. Are you sure this isn't too much for you?"

Jim paused his preparations to gather her hands in his. "I only had a touch of heatstroke, and Jo's tea has helped me regain my strength. Plus Deborah was here all day, serving up chicken broth and everything else. All that added with the strength your aura gives me, I'll be able to bring Ernest home."

She nodded and hugged him again.

Shoes secured, Jim put the badge into his front right pant pocket, his billfold in a back one, and his Colt into the jacket before joining the others in the parlor for a final goodbye.

A quarter of an hour later, Jo drove Jim's pickup truck well beyond the city limits. The headlights on the road barely illuminated the piercing darkness. Jim sat with his elbow propped on the passenger windowsill, drinking another jar of Jo's tea.

"It's difficult to believe Marie would stoop so low to capture a boy," Jim said at last.

"Ernest is a young man, Jim, and by all accounts, it looks like he went willingly."

That thought didn't improve his emotional state. After all Jim had done for Ernest, he hoped his son's choices would reflect a better upbringing than running away to work for Al Capone.

Jo pulled to a stop several dozen feet away from the gate to the Beauchamp house and cut the engine.

"How do you suppose we do this?" Jim asked.

"We check the manor. I'll communicate telepathically when needed, so listen for me." Jo's hand rested on Jim's on the seat between them. "You aren't without weapons—and I'm not talking about the revolver in your pocket. To protect yourself, imagine a halo of light around your body. You should be able to easily expand your aura from that."

Jim nodded and slowly opened the gate.

Jo strode across the expansive lawn lit by the nearly full moon. At the house, she peeked over the hedge through a front window before squatting down where Jim was hiding. "Ernest is in the parlor."

"Is he all right?"

"He's lounging on the sofa with Marie. He looks peaceful, but he's troubled. I don't think he wants to be here." As though knowing he was ready to bust through the door, Jo grabbed Jim by the shoulders to stop his hasty reaction. "Let me fly in and make sure no one else is here. Sit down so I can lean against you while I'm gone."

Jim huffed in annoyance over Jo forcing him to stay put while she did her Peeping Tom routine. Unable to sit still, he gently laid Jo's body on the ground before he slowly rose to peer in the window for himself. Seeing Ernest curled on his side like he'd slept as a young child cleared Jim's frustration about his recent behaviors like a deluge of a tropical storm washing the old wooden pieces of Government Street away in a flood.

He sank back to the ground and pulled Jo back upright beside him. It felt like he waited hours, but her hand soon lifted to pinch his cheek.

"Hey!"

"Shh," she hissed. "I've unlocked a back door."

"Let me do this part, Jo. I'm the one with the training and a gun."

She nodded and they stood in a crouch to go around the side of the house. The breakfast room they entered was dark, but Jo pointed the way. From the arched double doorway into the parlor, Jim glimpsed the top of Ernest's head on the arm of the sofa.

Jim walked into the room, gun drawn. "I'm here for my son."

After her initial surprise, Marie stood and flashed a beguiling smile. "Ernie's chosen my side over yours."

Grim-faced behind her from his seat on the sofa, Ernest briefly shook his head.

Drawing strength from his son's message, Jim stepped closer, his Colt pointing at Marie. "Your manipulation of a boy is nothing to the law, Marie. I'm taking him home."

"But I've grown fond of him. He'd be well-provided for here. What's that old saying about setting something that you love free? Ernest wants to leave your nest a few years early and I think you should let him."

A charged silence filled the room.

Ernest stood, and stepped away from Marie, whose smug countenance spoke of victory.

Try to stay calm, Jim. Jo's voice reached his mind.

Using the visualization she had taught him to control his fits of shellshock, he focused on his inner rhythm. Like a tide, the wave ran from head to toe, cresting near his heart with each beat.

Upon seeing Jo enter the room, Marie's countenance darkened. "You had to bring a witch with you, Jim?"

"It's only fitting since you abducted my best friend's son from my house." She crossed her arms.

"Ernest came willingly, Josephine. It's time everyone accepted that fact."

Seventeen

The sound of a door opening caused Ernest to look toward the entry hall. Ryan swaggered through arched doorway, hair disheveled and a cocky grin on his flushed face.

He stopped a few feet behind Ernest, putting the boy between himself and Jim who had moved the revolver to point halfway between Marie and Ryan.

"Officer Abbott paid us a call." Ryan stated. "And who's she?"

"His backup," Marie replied. "But she's only good for sharp word or two."

"I'm sorry for disappointing you, Ernest," Jim whispered. "If I had listened to you more, you might not be in this situation right now. I'm sorry I didn't do better."

Ernest stared at his father. His final sentences barely registered because Ernest stopped processing the information when he had opened with the words "I'm sorry." His birth father had never uttered that, and Jim Abbott—as much as he claimed not to be perfect—didn't usually allow his ego the bruising admitting mistakes made. His dad's steady gaze seared Ernest's soul into a remembrance of the compass points Miss

Eilands had prophesied about a few weeks before—truths wouldn't lead him astray. Ernest felt to his bones that Jim's love for him was the truest thing in his life.

While staring at his father, Marie rushed forward and plucked the revolver out of Jim's hand triumphantly. "Thank you for distracting him, Ernest."

Ryan snatched the gun from Marie and tucked it into the back of his belt. "Thank you both. And I've been wanting to do this since he parked that motorcycle in front of me."

Ryan punched Jim in the face and immediately rubbed his knuckles. "You've got a hard head."

A rivulet of blood ran out of Jim's left nostril as he swung back.

"Get away, Ernest!" Jim commanded as the pummeling continued.

"How am I going to explain these stains to Richard?" Marie asked above the noise of their fighting.

"With blood from yourself!" Miss Jo jumped at her.

Unsure who to help, Ernest looked from Miss Jo to his father and back. Seeing that Miss Jo already had Marie on the floor, he turned his focus to his dad, who had just smeared at the blood on his chin with his jacket sleeve as Ryan straightened after Jim's last blow.

Before Ernest registered what Ryan was doing, he pulled the Colt from his belt and pointed it at Jim. Ernest mentally grasped for control but couldn't completely capture Ryan's quick movement. Ryan squeezed the trigger. Ernest caused his arm to lower as the hammer fell, the shot echoing in the room. Flying too fast for Ernest to stop it, the bullet struck Jim's right hip with a crack.

Jim buckled with the impact.

"No!" Ernest flung Ryan against the far wall, the Colt falling to the floor in the process. Remorse over his choices sunk Ernest to his knees beside his father. "I didn't mean for you to die, Dad."

Ernest slowly turned him to lay on his back so he could see his face. Jim groaned with the movement. With a rush of hope, Ernest checked his hip. No blood was on him or the rug except where his face had been. But Ernest had seen the shot strike him. He visually searched the space around them, spying a spent bullet on the rug a few feet away, misshapen from impact.

"Dad?"

Jim's eyes opened. "Son."

Ernest picked up the lead and held it in front of him. "Did your aura shield you?"

"My hip feels…" Jim's right hand went to that area. He picked at a snag in the cloth of his pant pocket Ernest hadn't noticed, but he could tell his father felt something else. Jim's hand went inside the pocket and pulled out his badge. The shield shape had a pronounced dent near his badge number.

The guard Ernest had spied out front rushed in, gun in hand.

"What's going on?" His eyes darted around the room. Upon seeing Marie facedown on the rug, with Miss Jo holding both arms behind her and pressing a knee in her shoulder, he advanced.

Ernest concentrated on his father's Colt and slid it across the rug toward his side. The corner of Jim's mouth curled up behind his mustache with his smile as he reached for the weapon.

Ryan, recovered from hitting his head on the wall, fell in behind Orson's hulking figure.

"Get off of Marie, you bitch," Orson commanded.

Knowing better than to openly defy an armed man twice her size, Jo leapt to her feet and stepped aside at the same time Jim fisted his revolver.

"Marie, honey…" Orson reached out his free hand to help her move.

Ryan lunged for Orson's other hand, grabbing the gun.

As he turned toward Ernest with it, Jim steadily raised his Colt. Before Ryan could aim, Jim's shot struck him in the torso.

Orson immediately went for his fallen gun, but Ernest sent it into the unlit fireplace, where Jo was now standing, armed with a wrought iron poker from the hearth tool set.

Jim gingerly got to his feet, nodded at Miss Jo, then pointed his weapon toward Orson and Marie. "Marie, go see if there is anything to be done for Ryan. And you," he stared at Orson, "go sit on the sofa. Now where's the telephone?"

Marie pointed to the breakfast room as she walked toward Ryan, who was bleeding profusely from the stomach. Jim repocketed his badge and went to the rear archway, Ernest following close behind him to soak in the security he always radiated.

Jim asked the operator for the Mobile Police Station while keeping an eye on Orson. Once he got the shift lieutenant on the telephone, he explained about needing the sheriff's office sent to the Beauchamp house because of a death and the breakup of an Al Capone gambling den.

At his words, Orson began to rise. Jim lifted his arm so the man could see the Colt. The guard lowered himself back to the sofa with a sigh of resignation.

Within the next five minutes, Ryan took his last breath.

Marie was sent to an armchair near Miss Jo. Her darting eyes amid her pale face reminded Ernest of a scared mouse, but there were no feelings of pity for the treacherous woman. Miss Jo, and Orson looked at her more often than anyone else as Ernest's father slowly paced the room.

After minutes of grueling silence, Jim stepped toward Marie. "What happened to that sweet girl who was Winnie's best friend?"

"She grew up when she realized she'd never have everything she wanted in life." Marie held Jim's gaze for several seconds.

"You'll find no sympathy here. And as for your boss, I'm sure Capone will get word that things didn't work out here. Maybe he'll understand that Mobile wants nothing to do with his kind, so if he tries again it'll be across the state line in Mississippi."

"You look mighty proud of yourself, Officer Abbott." She lifted her chin. "With the news of you busting up a Capone operation, you'll be swaggering around town like the cake eater you used to be."

"This isn't about me." He scowled and motioned toward Ryan's body. "In case you forgot, you've got a dead teen over there."

"Yes, the one you murdered." When she smirked, Ernest saw the ugliness in her.

"He tried to kill me and then my son! There's nothing you can say that will change anything that happened here tonight."

"I didn't realize what he was capable of."

"Like hell you didn't! Save that pity card for a jury. You were completely aware what Ryan's history was around town."

"But at least it's not Ernie bleeding out."

"A life is a life, Marie." Jim stepped in front of Ernest, blocking his view of the woman. "Stop trying to feed us more lies. There isn't a promise in the world that will get me to trust you."

Eighteen

Jim refused to look at Marie, which was fine since Jo was guarding her, and glanced at Orson every few seconds to be sure he wasn't up to something. He kept pacing to keep his sore hip from growing stiff as the agonizingly slow minutes ticked by. The expanding scent of death caused Jim to swallow the bile that threatened to erupt, then he exhaled the toxic memories it nearly triggered.

To Jim's relief, when Chief Burch, the sheriff, and a handful of others arrived nearly an hour after the phone call, Orson and Marie were immediately contained.

In hopes of getting the ordeal over with, Jim started naming all the illegal activities that happened on the property. Standing in the middle of the room as he spoke, he tried to ignore the camera flash going off like small grenades as Ryan's body was photographed.

"Wait a second, Abbott," the chief interrupted him. "You were supposedly home sick. How'd you get involved with all this out here, including pulling the trigger on a kid?"

"If I may say something, Chief Burch," Jo said as she came to Jim's side, "Officer Abbott has placed himself in great peril tonight in order to save his son. He won't request it, but if you'd allow him to take a seat while he answers questions, it will be best for him."

"He does look pale," the chief remarked.

"And he's trembling. The heat exhaustion that struck him yesterday is nothing to take lightly."

Jo led Jim to the table in the breakfast room, and he whispered his thanks.

The opened back door allowed the heaviness of the pre-dawn to mix with the copper-tinged air. That hint of nature juxtaposed with the artificial coolness revitalized Jim enough to keep going.

A moment later, Ernest set a glass of water down in front of him. Jim drank, took a deep breath as the chief and sheriff settled across from him, then started on his story.

"Why didn't you warn us what was going on after you attended that party the other week?" the sheriff questioned.

"Knowing Commissioner Beauchamp was involved gave me pause as to what other public officials might be tangled up in things here," Jim replied. "I didn't want to place my family in jeopardy."

Chief Burch and the sheriff sized each other up while Jim finished drinking his water.

The sheriff cleared his throat. "I suppose that makes sense, but I don't like seeing Miss Marley in handcuffs. I'm sure Beauchamp used her as nothing more than trimming for the gambling den."

"She lured my son away," Jim stated. "Not to mention the other boy lying dead in there. She was a knowledgeable participant in the activities here."

"Miss Marley needs to stay in custody," the chief declared, "until all this is worked out. She could be an accessory to attempted murder, or should be charged with carnal knowledge at the very least since she hired that boy to guard a whorehouse."

The sheriff stood. "Let's see this gambling room since we're here."

"Gentlemen," Jo said as she stepped forward, "the Abbotts have had a trying night. If Jim's statement is all you need right now, could I please bring them home?"

"We need to get yours as well, Mrs. Harrington." The chief looked at Jim, then Ernest standing beside him. "Take your son outside, Abbott. We won't keep your friend too long."

"Thank you, Chief." Jim slowly stood, then placed a heavy hand on Ernest's shoulder. "Let me know if you need anything more from me."

In the back, Jim and Ernest settled beside each other on an iron bench.

"Can you forgive me?" Ernest's whisper was barely audible.

"Of course I can, son."

"I wanted to earn money to help me win Louisa."

"It's not the first time a young man lost his head over a pretty girl."

Ernest nodded, but Jim could tell there was more he wanted to say.

"It's upsetting when someone you respect lets you down," Jim said in hopes of giving Ernest another opening to speak.

"I thought Marie was my friend, but she was just using me."

"Ernest, don't take her scheming to heart. You're a fine young man. I'm sure any number of girls are gonna want you for a beau in the days ahead—possibly even Louisa Davenport."

"Especially if I make the baseball team."

Jim gently elbowed him. "Girls do like a man in uniform."

Ernest nodded.

"And more importantly, tonight proved how in tune you are with your soul. You know when you've done wrong and you made things right. Now that you've seen how people will try to exploit you to gain your power, you'll be that much more careful moving forward. I'm proud of you, Ernest."

"I'm sorry for everything, Dad."

"You're forgiven, son. And I hope you're ready to come home."

Ernest nodded and hugged him. Despite his exhaustion and discomfort, Jim felt that his life had been renewed.

***

As the day's golden light stretched over the canopy of oaks lining George Street Saturday morning, Jim and his family gathered around the kitchen table for one of Francesca's fabulous pancake breakfasts.

Baxter giggled when Ernest poured syrup over his food without touching the little maple jug.

Francesca playfully narrowed her eyes at him.

"What, Mom?" Ernest quipped. "It's the best way to keep my hands from getting sticky. Want some, Bax?"

"Yes!"

"I'll take some too, son." Jim winked at Francesca as his stack was covered.

She smiled and kissed Jim. "Y'all are incorrigible."

Knocking on the back screen door was accompanied by a man hollering for Jim.

"Come in, Happy!" Jim called out.

Officer Murphy's sturdy stride crossed the screened back porch. He entered with his uniform hat under his arm, newspaper in the other as Sunny rubbed against his boots.

"Morning, Abbotts. I brought your paper in."

They all replied with morning greetings, but the boys immediately tucked back into their syrupy stacks.

"Thanks, Happy." Jim stood and shook his hand before setting the newspaper on the counter.

"Could I get you a plate, Officer Murphy?" Francesca asked.

"No thanks, Miss Fran." He looked back to Jim. "I'm glad your neighbor happened by the other day. I guess I shouldn't have left you here alone that night, Abbott."

"It's nothing to fret over now. What brings you here?"

"After all the rumors I've heard since you missed work and then after Chief Burch got to the station yesterday, I wanted a visual on you myself to find out what was true."

Jim clapped him on the back and led him toward the porch so Baxter wouldn't overhear anything.

"What's the word?"

"That you'd been shot at the commissioner's house and since you were on your deathbed, the chief was finally going to promote you to detective because you helped bust a Capone ring, even if you killed a teenager."

Jim touched his bruised hip. "Three out of five ain't bad."

Officer Murphy rubbed his chin. "You aren't on your deathbed… but you were shot, Capone had a hold in Mobile County, and you killed a kid?"

"He was eighteen, and he tried to kill me previously and was aiming for Ernest when I got him." Jim shrugged off the heavy feeling. "But I wouldn't mind a promotion."

Brow raised, Officer Murphy nodded. "I bet, old man, though you know your winged brothers would miss you."

"Even if you become the senior member of the squadron?"

A huge grin painted his face. "On second thought, Abbott, you deserve a plainclothes job and a swell desk at the station."

They laughed, then Officer Murphy said he needed to report to work.

"Tell the guys hello for me. I'll be back on Monday."

"I'm glad your family is with you now, Abbott."

"So am I. Stay safe out there, Happy."

Jim kissed Francesca's cheek when he returned to the table.

"Is everything all right?" she asked as she rested a hand on his thigh.

"You remember those rumors Judge Spunner shared?" When she nodded, he continued. "The police department have some whoppers of their own going."

Francesca rolled her eyes. "I can imagine."

When they finished eating, the boys carried their dishes to the sink.

"How would you like to camp out in the backyard today, Bax?"

"We haven't done that in a long time!" Excitement painted Baxter's face.

"I'll rig up a blanket tent like I did last year and we can play games."

"Checkers?"

"Checkers it is, Bax." Ernest looked at Jim expectantly. "Do you want to play the winner, Dad?"

Grinning, Jim nodded. "I look forward to it, son."

THE END

Author's Note

Officer William "Happy" Murphy (plus traffic officers Green, Stout, and Harper) and Chief Burch are real names from 1927 at the Mobile Police Department. While the chief of police held his job for more than a decade after what is depicted in this book, Officer Murphy was tragically murdered in the line of duty during the pre-dawn hours of October 18, 1929. His life was taken when the speeding driver he pulled over on Broad Street shot him. At the age of thirty, Officer Murphy left behind his wife and three daughters. I had dedicated *Loyalty: Washington Square Secrets 3* in part to MPD's fallen officers, but I wanted to do a little more this time. Being able to feature Officer Murphy as a contemporary of fictional traffic/motorcycle officer Jim Abbott seemed like a fitting tribute for one of the three officers who lost their lives in the 1920s—tied with the 1990s and 2010s as the deadliest decades for the Mobile Police Department.

Officer Murphy's picture was part of twenty-two memorial photographs I saw each week on the Fallen Heroes board during my months at the Mobile Police Academy for the MPD's Citizens Police Academy course in the spring-summer of 2024. The twenty-one faces and one badge that represented the first fallen peace officer were humbling reminders of those who lost their lives while serving their community between 1872 and 2019. (NOTE: As of late April 2025, another MPD officer lost during the line of duty has been identified. Sergeant Phillips, in July 1864. Tracking the history of the department is an ongoing project due to incomplete files from over two centuries of service.)

Lieutenant Scott Congleton, leader of the MPD Police Academy for both citizens and police recruits during my time there, deserves a special shoutout. From the first evening, Lt. Congleton took all the class members' questions seriously, answering with candor and sincerity during a time of turmoil within MPD. The officers and staff of all ranks and units who taught at the Academy, and those I met on field trips, were exemplary ambassadors for the Mobile Police Department. And the five MPD beat officers I rode with in Precincts 1, 2, and 4 during my ride alongs (and their neighboring patrol officers we met up with on calls) were amazing to spend time with as I furthered my understanding of police officers during Class 33's course. And my appreciation also goes to Officer Wells, who I rode with in the autumn of 2024 and spring of 2025. While each officer is different, all are united in their desire to serve and protect the City of Mobile. It was a turbulent year for MPD, but they carried on.

Once again, Captain Billie L. Rowland assisted me with research and fact-checking for the Mobile Police Department in the 1920s, as well as completing early reads of the manuscript and rewritten sections. Even though I've dabbled with paranormal in the Washington Square Secret series, I still consider historical accuracy of upmost importance. Captain Rowland's efforts are always appreciated. Also, a special thank you to the spouses of law enforcement officers who took the time to answer my three-question survey so I could be sure my portrayal of family life with an MPD officer was authentic. Y'all are just as brave as those serving.

I enjoy incorporating my love of architecture into my stories by using historic homes in the Mobile, Alabama, area to house my people. Architect George B. Rogers is a long-time favorite of mine. I've used three of his houses in my other books and a fourth in a short story. Two of those houses are featured on the covers of *Tangled Discoveries* and *Severed Legacies* of The Malevolent Trilogy. The third is the Melling family's Government Street home, mentioned in this book, and a frequent setting throughout The Possession Chronicles.

In November of 2023, I was welcomed to Bishop Manor in South Mobile County. Owners Nancy and William Taylor gave me a tour of their George B. Rogers designed home. Plus they shared a myriad of photographs, articles, and verbal stories from the past they had gathered from previous owners and records about their property and surrounding acreage. Everything from a dairy to brothel to Al Capone was part of it. As you noticed, those tales (some verified, some not) sparked plenty of ideas for this book. Thank you, Taylor family, for allowing fictional Commissioner Richard Beauchamp and Sadie to host parties in your home that make the Roaring Twenties proud.

Bob Peck with the Historic Mobile Preservation Society's Minnie Mitchell Archives was a huge help in assisting me track down source material to verify last minute details while I was deep in edits during the fall of 2024. Thank you for your time and humor.

As always, I can't skip my critique partner, Candice Marley Conner, or beta reader Jennifer Lamont. Debbie Bradley joined their ranks this time with an early read too. They all offered great insights during pre-final edit reads and cheered me on when hashing out what needed to be done after editor Sean Connell got a hold of the manuscript. I've worked with Sean enough times now that I was able to pick out major things he would have valid issues with in *Betrayal,* so much so that I did my own overhaul on draft thirteen, rewriting ninety percent of it. After ten more rounds of edits, he still had a lot (understatement of the year) to sort out when I sent it to him. Thanks for being patient and willing to guide me, even when my characters run away with their angst.

And readers, many thanks to you. If you ever have questions about where the facts are verses the fiction or anything else, drop me an email or message on one of my social media pages. Find that information on the CONTACT page on my website. I'll catch you on the next literary adventure.

About the Author

Carrie Dalby has lived in Mobile, Alabama, since 1996, but called locations in both San Diego and Santa Cruz counties home while growing up in California. Serving two terms as president of Mobile Writers' Guild, five years as the Mobile area Local Liaison for the Society of Children's Book Writers and Illustrators, and helping coordinate the Mobile Literary Festival are just a few of the writing-related volunteer positions she's held. When Carrie isn't reading, writing, researching, or browsing bookstores, libraries, estate sales, thrift stores, museums, or archives, she can often be found volunteering with the Mobile Citizens Police Academy Alumni Association or attending concerts.

Carrie writes for both teens and adults. *Fortitude* is listed as a "Best Historical Book for Kids" by Grateful American Foundation for its historical accuracy and reader engagement for those in grades fifth through tenth. As of 2025, The Possession Chronicles, The Malevolent Trilogy, and Washington Square Secrets are her Southern Gothic series for adults. She has also published several shorts that can be found in different anthologies as well as her short story collection *Masked Flaws and Other Stories.*

For more information, social media links, newsletter sign-up, and more, visit Carrie Dalby's website:

carriedalby.com